Of All The Rotten Luck.

Carrie was wearing her oldest work clothes, and they were drenched with perspiration, caked with dust. That wasn't all her boots were caked with, either. Fly-tagging a herd of cows was dirty business. And now she'd run straight into Rex Ryder for the first time in ages.

For years she'd savored every scrap of news she could glean about Rex. She'd always hoarded a secret dream that one day she'd run into him again, and he would fall madly in love with her and beg her to forgive him. When her younger sister had started dating Rex's brother, Carrie had had one more reminder of Rex. That was when she'd finally come to terms with reality. Rex didn't want her.

He hadn't wanted her all those years ago, and didn't want her now. Otherwise he would have come back for her. It wasn't as though Rex didn't know where to find her. She had been here, having his baby, making a dry-eyed deal to marry a man she didn't love, just to give her and Rex's baby a father...the baby Rex had never known existed.

Dear Reader:

Believe it or not, it's been ten years since Silhouette Desire first made its way from us, the publisher, to you, the readers! And what a wonderful ten years it's been. Silhouette Desire stories are chock-full of delicious sensuality combined with deep emotions. Silhouette Desire is romance at its finest.

To celebrate this decade of delight, I'm proud to present our JUNE GROOMS, six stories about men and marriage. Each of these stories is unique: some are about men who marry—and some are about men whose main goal in life is to *avoid* wedded bliss! But all of these romances concern men who finally meet their match in one special woman.

The authors involved are some of the finest that Silhouette Desire has to offer: Ann Major, Naomi Horton, Raye Morgan, Suzanne Simms, Diana Palmer (with the next installment of her MOST WANTED series!) and Dixie Browning (with a terrific *Man of the Month!*). Some of these stories are serious; some are humorous—all are guaranteed to bring you hours of reading pleasure.

As an extra special treat, these six authors have written letters telling what they like about Silhouette Desire and discussing their feelings about romance . . . and marriage.

These books are our anniversary presents to you, our readers. I know you'll enjoy reading JUNE GROOMS as much as I did. And here's to the *next* ten years!

Sincerely,

Lucia Macro
Senior Editor

DIXIE BROWNING

BEST MAN FOR THE JOB

SILHOUETTE *Desire*®

Published by Silhouette Books New York

America's Publisher of Contemporary Romance

For my own cowgirl.
Remember Whitney? And Martha?

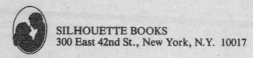

SILHOUETTE BOOKS
300 East 42nd St., New York, N.Y. 10017

BEST MAN FOR THE JOB

Copyright © 1992 by Dixie Browning

ISBN: 0-373-05720-2

First Silhouette Books printing June 1992

All the characters in this book have no existence outside the imagination of the author and have no relation whatsoever to anyone bearing the same name or names. They are not even distantly inspired by any individual known or unknown to the author, and all incidents are pure invention.

Printed in the U.S.A.

DIXIE BROWNING

has written over forty books for Silhouette since 1980. She is a charter member of the Romance Writers of America and an award-winning author and has toured extensively for Silhouette Books. She also writes historical romances with her sister under the name Bronwyn Williams.

Dear Friends,

Once every few years I have an opportunity to say a few personal words to you. As usual, there are so many things I want to talk about, so many questions I want to ask you, that I don't know where to begin. We have so much in common, you and I. The very fact that you read romances at all means you have a strong streak of idealism, not to mention optimism—which means you're the kind of person I enjoy getting to know.

If you read Silhouette Desire books, then that means you're not only a romantic, you're also a realist. Not only do you enjoy reading about that special magic that can happen between a certain man and a certain woman, but you're mature enough to enjoy stories about today's people meeting the special challenges of today's problems.

Don't you love the stories written these past few years, when we've been allowed to explore the male point of view? Remind me to tell you sometime what it's like to get inside a man's head and see the world through his eyes!

Speaking of heroes, like women's shoes, they come in a variety of sizes, shapes, colors and styles (no heels, of course). My heroes tend to be chosen more for comfort than style, but I'd like to believe their style suits more than a few women.

I've yet to meet the perfect man (my mother-in-law's opinion notwithstanding). The real fun comes in matching the strengths and weaknesses of different men and women. The hero I chose for *Best Man for the Job,* Rex Ryder, is not *quite* perfect, which is what makes him so *very* perfect for Carrie Lanier... who also isn't quite so perfect.

But then, I expect you know exactly what I'm talking about, don't you?

Keep in touch,

Dixie Browning

One

___

Rex stood in the doorway of the pink-and-gray room that had once been his father's office and stared at the elegant, emaciated blonde in the pink silk lounging pajamas. Stella Lowrie Ryder had changed little in all the years since she'd married his father. She had to be in her middle fifties now, even though she appeared a good ten years younger. And beautiful. Oh, yes, Stella was beautiful by any man's standards, but even as a child Rex had been repelled by the coldness of her pale blue eyes. Expecting little from his stepmother, he had seldom been disappointed.

She'd been mixing herself a drink when Rex showed up. "Help yourself." She nodded to the ornate Chinese liquor cabinet.

"No, thanks." It was barely noon. "Is Belinda going to be here this weekend?" he asked.

"She's tied up with the Junior League rummage sale."

Rex felt a mixture of relief and guilt. He had never had much in common with his older sister—not even their parents. Rex had been adopted by John Ryder and his first wife. But that didn't keep Belinda, who was six years older than he, from trying to run his life. As personnel director for a major firm, Belinda had a proclivity for pushing people around, and that included her family. "What about Billy?" Rex had been looking forward to seeing his younger half brother.

"Out."

"Out?" Rex repeated. "Did you tell him I was coming?"

"I might've forgotten, I don't know. Do you want a drink, or are you just going to stand there glowering at me?"

Rex bit off a sharp comment. He and Stella had tangled before. It never solved anything. "You want to take a guess where he is?"

Stella shrugged her fashionably bony shoulders and sipped her Scotch and water. "Probably out celebrating. He breezed through his first year at Duke, in case you didn't know." Her gaze sparkled with malice, which Rex ignored.

"I knew," Rex replied quietly. Breezed was hardly the word Rex would have chosen, but he did know the kid had squeaked by. He knew, too, that Stella would never let him forget that he himself had been kicked out of three boarding schools by the time he was fifteen. The fact that he had finally managed to accumulate a law degree, besides one in criminal justice, as well as associate degrees in police procedure, computer science and statistical analysis meant nothing to Stella, since he'd done it on his own, without her money or her blessings. "You think he might be somewhere on campus?"

"Who knows?"

"And who cares, right? Maternity always did become you, Stella. You're such a caring person."

"Thank you, love, you're too kind." She slammed her drink down on the drum table. "Oh, for lord's sake, he's probably out with that little Lanier girl. She's been pestering him all year!"

Turning slowly, Rex stared at her. "Lanier? Ralph Lanier's daughter?"

"I don't keep up with the genealogy of every little tramp in the woods."

"Red hair?" God, it couldn't be Carrie! Billy was just a kid, and Carrie would be, what? Thirty? Besides, Carrie was...

"I haven't the faintest idea what color her hair is. It's probably full of hayseeds, whatever the color, but I can tell you this much—if she thinks she's going to get her greedy little hooks into *my* son, she's in for a disappointment! My plans for Billy don't include letting him get trapped by some greedy little nobody fresh off the farm."

Carrie Lanier. Memories flooded in before Rex could clamp the lid on. Carrie's daughter? No. Oh, hell no! Her children couldn't be that old. And besides, her name wouldn't be Lanier any longer.

"Come to think of it, wasn't that the name of the girl you were so hot and bothered about back in high school? I seem to remember some redheaded thug in bib overalls storming in here to warn John that his rutting bastard of a son was going to wind up singing soprano if he ever came near his daughter again. Would this be the same charming family, by any chance? They must breed like rabbits if they have a daughter Billy's age, too."

Stella shot a curious look at her stepson, taking in the breadth of his shoulders, the lean flanks and those wicked-looking eyes. God, he was a marvelous piece of work! Who would ever had dreamed that the sullen little brat he'd been when Stella had married the newly widowed John Ryder would turn out like this? He'd been shockingly attractive as a teenager, but totally unmanageable. There'd never been any love lost between the two of them, but the final break had come when he'd tried to interfere in the way she was raising Billy, who was no blood kin of his at all, as she'd reminded him more than once.

"I hear you and that friend of Belinda's, Maddie Stone, are getting pretty serious. Who are her people?"

"Mr. and Mrs. Stone," Rex replied dryly, knowing full well what Stella was digging for.

"I hope they can afford a big wedding. Belinda's already making plans and checking the club for open dates."

"I wouldn't go buying any wedding gifts just yet. Bel's been trying to organize my life since I was in kindergarten. She knows when to back off." Rex and his sister had an understanding. She meddled and he ignored her. "If Billy comes in, tell him I'll be at the cabin all week and to call me, will you?"

"If I think of it, and if he shows up."

"Which pretty well spells out my chance of seeing him, right? Where does he hang out? Where does he usually take the Lanier girl on a date—to a movie? A club?"

Stella shrugged. "The nearest haystack, probably."

Rex muttered something under his breath and turned to stare out the tall window at the flawlessly groomed box-woods. The damned place suffocated him! Stella had inherited it after the first poor devil she'd married had popped off with a heart attack. She hadn't been about to give it up to move into the Ryders' shabby barn of a house. Instead, John Ryder, his seven-year-old adopted son and his thirteen-year-old daughter had moved into Stella's small mansion.

As a child, Rex had hated it. As a man, he still did. "When Billy shows up, ask him to give me a call, will you?"

Some half an hour later he unlocked the door of the cabin he had built with his own two hands on the rugged riverside tract his father had left him. Throwing open a few windows, he wondered why he'd expected anything more from his talk with his stepmother. He and Stella had never agreed over the way she was raising her son. It had been bad enough before John Ryder's fatal plane crash. For all her outward fragility, Stella had been more than a match for her charming, easygoing second husband.

It had been Rex who had taught the boy to fight back when the other kids called him a pansy. Taught him to hunt, to get down and dirty, and to swear when the occasion demanded.

Stella put Billy in the charge of a nanny who saw that he stayed clean, said yes ma'am and no ma'am, and practiced his piano lessons for an hour every day. Once or twice a week, Stella ordered him to be dressed up so that she could show him off before her friends at the club. When Rex had protested, she had told him what he could do.

A few years later, he had done it, but not on account of Billy. He'd left because of Carrie. Left and vowed to make a place for himself and come back for her in five years; but by the time he got back, it was already too late.

Why not give in to Belinda's unsubtle hints that Maddie would make him the perfect wife? At least it would put an end to all those ancient dreams that refused to die a natural death.

Standing in the open door, Rex stared down toward the river, his view obscured by dense woods and a bank of wild mountain laurel. More than once, a long time ago, he'd come close to heaven in the middle of that same laurel slick.

Maybe he should have invited Maddie along, after all. He had turned down her invitation to go to the beach, claiming he needed to check on his property. The trouble was, lately he'd had the feeling she was expecting something more from their comfortable arrangement. Something he wasn't ready to offer. She'd even conned him into looking at houses with her!

But then, the woman was a realtor. Just because he never discussed his work with her, that was no reason she had to tiptoe around when it came to discussing her own career. If that's all it was...

Oh, hell, he was getting paranoid! Belinda had been trying to fix him up with one or another of her female friends ever since she realized that he wasn't going to wind up as a jailbird after all. He kept expecting to wake up one morning and find himself being hauled off to church with a ring in his nose.

The generator cranked up after the third try, and Rex went back inside and switched on a light. The place wasn't as musty as he'd expected. It had been several months since he'd had enough free time to make it worthwhile opening up. With a couple of weeks comp time on his hands, he'd been looking forward to inviting Billy out for a few days of man-to-man stuff. What with Billy's school and Rex's work, it had been awhile. He missed the closeness they'd once shared, but it was too much to hope it could last. Not only were they not real brothers, there was a dozen years separating them.

Rex breathed deeply of the warm, woodsy smells all around him. First priority was to slow down and soak up some much-needed relaxation. The last time he'd been out to the cabin, he'd brought along his laptop and a stack of files two feet high, and ended up cutting short his time here to get back to the office and start crunching numbers on the mainframe.

This time he'd been a little smarter. He'd brought along his overnight bag, his shaving kit, a bottle of Scotch and a stack of paperback books. He gazed around at the simply furnished, masculine interior of his comfortable hideaway, feeling some of the tension begin to seep away, and then he did a double take.

Was that a champagne bottle on the counter? And *panty hose?* Where the hell had *they* come from?

He dropped the empty bottle into the trash bag, which was half-filled—something else he couldn't take credit for. Scowling at the offending scrap of nylon draped over the back of his massive leather sofa, he stalked across the pine floor and threw open the bedroom door. He might not be the world's best housekeeper, but he knew damned well he hadn't gone off and left the bed unmade!

The drone of the generator muffled his curses as he picked up a chewing gum wrapper from the floor. Chewing gum and champagne. That sounded like Billy.

But the *panty hose?*

Cursing tiredly, Rex tossed the gum wrapper into the partially filled trash basket. It didn't take a degree in police procedure to figure out that Billy was using the cabin as a convenient trysting place.

"Dammit, boy," Rex muttered. "The position of black sheep in the Ryder family was filled before you were out of short pants. Why'd you have to go fooling around with—"

Deliberately, he clamped the lid on his irritation. Carrie Lanier was ancient history, and regardless of who the girl in question was, it was none of his business. Billy was old enough to take care of himself.

Rex finished opening the windows and putting in the screens and then switched on the gas refrigerator. The pantry was all but empty. He was going to have to lay in a few groceries. He should have done it on his way out of town, but he'd been so steamed over Stella's attitude. First she crippled the boy with overprotection, and then she rejected any offer of masculine guidance. It would serve her right if her baby got himself in trouble with some little bimbo and had to marry her!

Only it wouldn't serve the girl right. Shotgun weddings had gone out of style, but these days there were worse things out there to worry about. Just how responsible was his baby brother, anyway?

They needed to talk, and soon, from the looks of things. This time Rex wasn't going to pull any punches. This was the real world, not just a practice game. Screw up, and you just might find yourself thrown off the team for keeps.

A drift of something sweet and spicy blew through the windows, and he inhaled deeply, telling himself that he might as well relax while he could, there was nothing to be done at the moment. He would call Stella's place later and see if he could catch Billy on the run, but meanwhile, he might as well lay in a supply of groceries.

Locking the door behind him, Rex backed his low-slung 850-i around and took aim at the rutted uphill driveway.

"Son of a—!" He slammed on the brakes as a battered pickup truck came barreling over the top of the hill. In a cloud of red dust, the two vehicles came to rest less than four feet apart. "Are you *crazy or something?*" he roared, catapulting out of the driver's seat.

His jaw dropped and he stared at the small figure that ejected from the rusty red cab. Even after nine years, there was no mistaking that wild crop of bullfighting red hair. Or that stacked and packed little body in the faded jeans.

The last time he'd seen her she'd been wearing jeans, too. She'd been steering a grocery cart across Fowler's parking lot, with a dark-haired kid hanging on to her hand, crying for "Mama, Mama," to go back and buy something or other.

Rex had felt like cursing. He'd felt like crying. Instead, he'd driven off, bought himself a bottle of bourbon and got howling, knee-walking drunk. It hadn't helped, but at least he'd forgotten the pain of losing her while he'd coped with the worst hangover in his entire life.

After a while, the memories had begun to fade. But one thing obviously hadn't faded. Carrie's temper! If tiny clenched fists and eyes the color of bittersweet chocolate could kill, he'd be a dead man.

"Where is she?" Carrie demanded. Her voice was the same, too. Husky, with a firm undertone.

Recovering his wits, Rex said, "Where's who?"

"Don't give me that, damn you, what have you done with her?"

"Nice to see you again, too, Carrie. How've you been? You still live around these parts?"

Carrie struggled to contain the fear and anger that had risen to explosive levels. Sooner or later it had been bound to happen. The wonder was that it had taken fourteen years and ten months. "Don't hand me that, Rex Ryder, you know very well what I'm talking about. Where's my sister? I know Kim's been coming out here. I warned her about that boy a hundred times, but she just won't listen!"

"You've lost your sister and you think I've got her cooped up here in my cabin, is that what you're saying?"

That blew the cork. Carrie charged across the intervening distance, her booted feet negotiating the rough ground with practiced ease until she stood toe-to-toe with the handsome bastard she'd spent half her life dreaming about. "You know damned well what I mean! You and that irresponsible brother of yours! Now step aside before I run you down!''

She paused for breath, her full bosom heaving tumultuously. She'd expected Billy. Billy she could handle, but Rex was another matter.

Oh, blast, he was even more stunning than she remembered, Carrie thought hopelessly. After so long, didn't a person build up immunity?

She answered her own question. No woman could be immune to a man like Rex Ryder. It was more than a matter of hormones; it cut bone deep. Once exposed, the disease was inevitable, and there was no cure. And Carrie had been exposed. God, had she ever been exposed!

Leveling him with a quelling look, she forced herself to ignore everything above and below his Adam's apple. ''Are they still inside?''

Rex held up his hands, palm out. She could feel the heat of him, and she stepped back, nearly tripping on the rough ground. When he reached out to her, she brushed his hand away. ''Rex, I'm warning you—Billy was bad enough, but if the pair of you have—''

''Hold on there—I've never even laid eyes on your sister! I don't know where she is. I don't even know where Billy is. If it's any comfort to you—''

''Comfort!'' she yelled. Too furious for caution, she wrenched her eyes up from his Adam's apple, past his square jaw, past the mouth that had once melted her to the very core, past his beautiful, imperfect nose, to clash head-on with a pair of slate-colored eyes.

Her shoulders drooped. It wasn't fair. It just wasn't fair! ''Look, I don't know what's going on, but I do know that Daddy's fit to be tied. Kim didn't come home last night. She only just turned eighteen yesterday, and if that brother of yours has done anything to hurt her, he's going to have to answer to me!''

Which was a hell of a lot better than answering to Ralph Lanier, as Rex could personally attest. He wondered if her father had ever told her about threatening to geld him all those years ago.

He'd never got to tell her. Lanier and that hard case backing him up with a pitchfork had seen to that, but he'd thought she would understand. They had been so crazy about each other back then, unable to stay apart, risking everything to steal away and meet on the wild acres across the river from the Lanier's farm.

But Rex's own mother had been fifteen when she'd had him, according to John Ryder. She had died in childbirth. And as wild as Rex had been back then, there was no way he could let Carrie go on taking the same risks until they were old enough to marry. When his father had confronted him with Lanier's charges, he had told him they were engaged. Furious, John Ryder had shipped him off to work in a friend's logging camp on the West Coast. He had worked his tail off, done some growing up, and got a start on a degree. Working days, studying nights, he had made plans to go back for her. He'd written, and waited for a reply. And then waited some more.

How long had she waited after he'd left? The kid she'd had in tow when he'd finally made it back had been three or four years old. She couldn't have been more than twenty-one at the time. How many did she have now? Who had she married? Who took her to bed every night and sated himself with the woman Rex had thought of as his own all those years?

"Well? I'm waiting for an explanation! Where are they?"

"I don't have one. They're not here. I don't know where they are, or if they're even together. Stella mentioned—''

"I can imagine what your stepmother mentioned. She hates Kim."

"I wasn't aware that they'd ever met. Stella doesn't keep tabs on all Billy's friends," he said, trying to be diplomatic.

Diplomacy was the last thing on his mind when every cell in his body was saturated with the sight of her, the scent of her. Memories flooded back until he had to shake his head to clear it. "Look, Carrie, I don't know if she's with him or not, but they're probably both old enough to know what they're doing. Billy's twenty-one." An immature twenty-one, he added silently. Insulated by too much money and spoiled rotten by a doting mother. "You say your sister's eighteen—"

"A very young eighteen," Carrie amended.

She looked so small, so lost, so worried. Rex wanted to offer comfort, but how could he? He didn't know where that pair was, or what they were up to. "Look, she's probably home waiting for you right now. You're probably all upset over nothing."

Red flags of temper flared in her cheeks, and she chopped the air with her fists. Carrie always talked with her hands. "Don't patronize me! She's not home! I just left there!"

Rex grabbed her by the shoulders, meaning only to slow her down to a reasonable speed. "Whoa, lady. Cool down a little before you explode."

Unfortunately, he had miscalculated the effect touching her would have on him. He caught her wrists, using his thumbs to open her fists. When they ended up pressed into her palms, she tried to wrench away.

"I don't have time to cool down! Lib said Kim wasn't in her room, and that her bed hadn't been slept in and no one knows where she is! Daddy will kill her if I don't find her and get her home!"

She tried to wriggle free, but his fingers only tightened. A pair of purple finches set up a warbling squabble in a nearby pine tree, and Carrie bit her lip, wishing she hadn't gone racing off quite so fast. She was wearing her oldest work clothes, and they were drenched with perspiration, caked with dust. That wasn't all her boots were caked with, either. Fly-tagging a herd of cows was dirty business.

And she had to run smack-dab into Rex again! Of all the rotten luck! For years she had savored every scrap of news she could glean about him, even when she'd been married to Don. Especially then! She had heard Rex had been living on the West Coast, but a few years ago someone had said he'd come back to North Carolina and was working in Raleigh, and from then on, she'd hoarded a secret dream that one day she would run into him again, and he would fall instantly in love with her and beg her to forgive him.

When Kim had started dating Billy, she'd had one more reminder of Rex. As if she'd needed it by then. That was when she had finally come to terms with reality. Rex didn't want her. He hadn't wanted her all those years ago, and he didn't want her now. Otherwise he would have come back. It wasn't as if he didn't know where to find her. She had been there, having his baby, making a dry-eyed deal to marry a man she didn't love just to give her child a father.

Rex watched the play of emotions on her face. Only by exercising the utmost control was he able to keep from hauling her ripe little body into his arms and kissing the living daylights out of her. Just barely. Time hadn't diminished her fiery splendor. If anything, it had enhanced it. At fifteen, Carrie had been a remarkable combination of guts and vulnerability in a tiny, voluptuous package. As a mature woman, she was...

Splendid was the word that came to mind. He cleared his throat. "Okay, let's take it step-by-step," he said calmly.

"Step-by-step!" she exploded. Her hand sliced through the air again. "Do you have any idea what's been going on?"

"No, but I suspect you're about the enlighten me."

"I'll enlighten you, all right. That brother of yours has been sneaking out here to this—this *cabin* of yours, with my sister! That's what's been going on!"

"If you didn't approve, why didn't you put a stop to it?"

"I just found out, that's why! I called everyone I could think of, and believe me, I learned more than I wanted to know!"

"About your sister?"

"About you Ryder men," she accused. "Not that it came as any great surprise, believe me. I thought Billy was wild, but everybody in three counties knows about you and your conquests—not that I wanted to hear any of it, because I couldn't care less how many women you—you—"

"Lay?" Rex offered gently. He'd always loved seeing her riled, which was most of the time. "Enjoy?"

"Stop bragging, you're downright disgusting!"

"I haven't changed, Carrie. One of the things I liked best about you was that you never judged me by what other people said about me."

She was staring fixedly at the middle button of his white shirt, which hadn't fared too well in the June heat and humidity. Her eyes were dry, but the tip of her short nose was red, which was a dead giveaway. Rex had been a Carrie-watcher since his first few days at Durham County High. She had transferred over from Orange County the same year Rex had got himself kicked out of St. Andrews, and had finally talked his father into letting him attend the county schools.

Carrie's father had taken her out of her own school when some young stud had started making a pest of himself, and transferred her to Durham County. Rex could almost sympathize with the poor jerk. Carrie's body had matured before she was emotionally equipped to handle the attention it commanded. In the first week at her new school she'd had a few run-ins with some of the older boys.

Rex had watched her deal with half a dozen toughs using a hard right, a sharp-toed boot, and a tongue that could sting like a swarm of yellow jackets. A rebel and an outsider himself, he had admired her courage even more than her skill. From then on, he'd kept an eye on little Carrie Lanier in case she came up against something she couldn't handle.

She never had, at least not until that day beside the river. But that had been a year later.

"Carrie, listen to me," he said now. "If they're together, it's because they want to be." Carefully, he replaced his hands on her shoulders. "Your sister's old enough to look out for herself, honey. So is Billy." He wished he could be sure of that.

"Oh? How old does a girl have to be to look out for herself these days? Twelve? Fifteen?"

Rex's face took on a new harshness. They were no longer talking about her sister and his brother. The awareness hung in the pulsating heat that surrounded them. Carrie had been fifteen that spring. He had known it, but it had suited him to forget it. Before he'd known what was happening, they were in over their heads.

"Carrie?" he said quietly. "Why didn't you answer my letter?"

She sent him a suspicious glance. "What letter?"

"I wrote from Oregon."

"I never got it."

Ralph Lanier. He might've known. "I came back to see you nine or ten years ago, but by then it was already too late."

Too late. Carrie's breath caught in her throat. Rex moved his hands down her arms, reminding her that he was still holding her captive, and she wrenched away. "I can't imagine what you're talking about, but whatever it is, it doesn't matter. All that matters now is Kim."

Right. Dropping her hands, Rex stepped back. "Look, I'll talk to Billy when I see him again, but you may as well know, I don't have a whole lot of influence with him anymore. Not that I ever did."

"Oh, I'm sure you did. You were the big hero, didn't you know? Every boy's favorite role model."

"God forbid," Rex said feelingly.

"After you left town, half the boys in Durham County High took to wearing black tees, black jeans and black engineer's boots. If they could make their hair flop down over their foreheads the way yours used to do, they did that, too. It was enough to make a body sick!"

"I'm sure it was. I apologize, if that helps any."

"Yes, well . . . they got over it soon enough."

And you, Carrie . . . did you get over it, too? Over me?

Time shimmered into infinity, accompanied by the drone of insects and the lazy whisper of the river to the rocks as they stared at each other. Rex was the first to recover. "Carrie, about Billy and your sister . . . I don't know what's going on, but you have my promise to look into it. I left word with Stella for Billy to call as soon as he gets in. When he does, I'll pass the word to cool it with your sister, okay?"

Carrie screwed up her small face in concentration. "I was just so sure they'd be here. Are you positive—?"

"The place was shut up tight when I got here half an hour ago. There was an empty champagne bottle, a gum wrapper and a pair of panty hose in the—"

"Panty hose!"

He held up a soothing hand. "Now that doesn't necessarily mean what you're thinking. It could just mean that the last time they were here, they decided to, ah . . . go wading in the river."

"No way. Not Kim. She hates squishy bottoms."

A vision of a tiny, voluptuous redhead reaching for a wildflower and slithering down a slippery riverbank rose vividly before his eyes. She'd landed with a splash and come up sputtering and swearing before he could even kick off his shoes. Remembering, Rex banked the fires that had arisen along with the memory of that day so long ago.

She'd been fifteen then, which made her thirty now. She wore it beautifully. "Look, I promise I'll check it out, okay?"

She sighed, and his eyes were drawn to her magnificent bosom. "When, next week? Next month? Just forget it," she said, turning away. "I'll do it myself."

She was halfway to her truck before Rex caught her. Spinning her around, he demanded, "What do you mean, forget it?"

Eyeing the square, tanned hand on her arm, Carrie said pointedly, "It doesn't even bother you, does it? I guess it's different with men, but dammit, I won't have a spoiled brat like Billy Ryder ruining my sister's whole future! She deserves better, even if she is too young to realize it."

Already tired, Rex had been jerked around just about enough for one day. "Oh, is that right? Well, let me tell you something, honey, your little sister wouldn't be the first girl who thought she could trade a little sack time for a—"

Carrie swung at him, but Rex grabbed her fist before it could connect. "Let me go! My sister's not like that!"

"No? Then you tell me—what's Billy's great appeal? His looks? His brains? His charming manners? Hell no, it's his mama's bankroll, and you damn well know it!"

Carrie jerked her wrist away. Blinded by tears of anger, she stalked across the dried ruts, flung open the door of her truck and climbed inside.

Rex let her go. There wasn't much else he could do, but dammit, why did it have to be *her* sister? Why couldn't Billy have picked on some other girl? He winced as she took out two laurel bushes and a nice clump of wild fern in turning around. Maybe he should have kept her here until she cooled down enough to drive.

Ah, hell, let her husband worry about her. He'd wasted too much time on her already, and she wasn't worth it. They'd both been too young to know what they were doing back then. Good thing for both of them that he'd had sense enough to get out before things had got entirely out of hand.

Instead of going out for supplies, Rex got on the phone. Stella was out, according to the housekeeper. He left word for Billy to call the minute he got in. Then, he got a list of several numbers where Billy might be located. Friends. A frat house. A local hangout.

No luck. No one had seen him, no one knew where he was. "But hey, he was asking if any of the guys had a map of South Carolina," one of Billy's friends offered. "I don't know if that's any help."

Rex assured the boy that it was definitely of help. "You're sure it was of South Carolina? Billy's mother has a place at Hilton Head. I'd have thought he could find his way blindfolded by now."

"Yeah, man, I'm sure. I lent him a map I got when I went to Charleston to visit my girl. So what's going down? Billy in some kind of trouble?"

"No trouble, just a case of mixed signals, that's all."

Rex replaced the phone, deep in thought. The beach, huh? It was a possibility, all right, but why would he need a map?

He tried to tell himself that with or without the girl, there wasn't much anyone could do about it now. They were both of age. On the other hand, Billy was still pretty immature. He'd suffered all his life from a surplus of money and a deficit of parental guidance.

Funny how two men could be so different at the same age. At twenty-one, Billy was still a kid. At the same age, Rex had been well on the way to living down his early reputation as a tough kid who would probably end up in jail. The rep had been well deserved. He had deliberately cultivated it. There was a certain irony in the fact that he had ended up working for the North Carolina Department of Justice.

In spite of his notoriety, he and Carrie had found a lot in common. They'd both been rebels, they'd both been loners, neither of them interested in joining any of the school organizations. They'd both had much younger siblings, and both had lost their mothers. In Rex's case, he'd lost two—his birth mother and his adoptive mother. Carrie's mother had run off and left a husband and two daughters, which in a way, he supposed, was even more painful.

There was also the fact that Rex's father had owned the property on the other side of the river from the Lanier farm. One way or another, the Ryders and the Laniers seemed fated to tangle. Who knows what might have happened, Rex mused, if Carrie had been a little older and he'd been a little less wild?

At the moment, however, Carrie wasn't his problem. Billy was. Because the more he thought about it, the less he liked it. There was a lot of trouble out there just waiting for some half-baked kid with too much money and not enough judgment. Fresh out of his first year at Duke, Billy was ripe for it.

"Ah, hell," he muttered, and reached for the phone again.

He ran a routine check on Billy's PIN number, which included police, morgue, hospitals and any charges that had been turned in. He drew a blank. Which didn't mean the kid wasn't in trouble. It only meant that the trouble hadn't been reported yet.

Another couple of calls produced similar results, and Rex leaned back in his chair and stroked his jaw, which was already beginning to feel like sandpaper. He had one last option. A hacker he knew in Durham. He looked up the number and placed a call, outlined the situation and hung up. A few minutes later he was headed out to top off his tank and check the levels. That done, he called back, using his car phone. "Nothing? Are you sure? Did you run down—"

"Yep. All the usual and then some. The works. The kid's clean as a whistle. Either he knows he's being scanned and is using cash, or he's keeping his nose clean and his wallet in his pocket. Adds up to the same thing. Zip."

Rex massaged his left temple. The ragged edge of a headache reminded him that he hadn't eaten since six that morning. "Yeah, sure."

"Sorry, Ryder. Wish I could help you. I'll keep an eye out. Check in again if you don't find him, right?"

"Right. And thanks, Steve."

Back to square one.

* * *

"Lib, is she home yet?" By the time the screen door slammed behind her, Carrie was halfway through the kitchen. The housekeeper, Lib Swanson, glanced up from the shirt she was mending and shoved her glasses up on top of her salt-and-pepper curls. There was a look of compassion on her face, which Carrie forced herself to ignore. A little sympathy and she just might fall apart, and that was the last thing any of them needed.

"Sorry, honey. I haven't heard anything new."

"Where's Daddy? He came in for lunch, didn't he?"

"Right after you left. I made him lie down for a spell. It's too hot for a body to go chasing all over creation in a contraption that doesn't even have a sunshade."

Ralph Lanier was paralyzed from the waist down. A mechanic who used to work on the farm had refitted an old golf cart with hand controls and balloon tires, thus enabling Ralph to get around. He'd planned to put a cab on it, but Ralph had been too impatient to wait. It was both a blessing and a curse, as they worried constantly that he would get into trouble tooling around the rough terrain of the three-hundred-forty-acre farm, but there was no holding him back. Lib, who had been with them for years, had more influence than either Kim or Carrie, and that was little enough.

"You're just going to have to handle Daddy for me. I've got an idea Kim might've taken off for Myrtle Beach. Remember she wanted me to give her a week there with a friend for her birthday?"

"Doesn't want much, does she? That little lady's getting too big for her britches."

Carrie knew all too well that her sister was spoiled. Part of the blame was her own, but how could she be expected to devote the time needed to keep Kim in line when she had her own daughter to look after and the farm to run?

"If I thought Rex would... No, I'd better do it myself."

The housekeeper's attractive face perked up at the mention of Rex. She'd been with them ever since Kim was a baby, which meant the family had few secrets from her. At times Carrie thought Lib suspected that Joanna wasn't Don's child, but if she had any such suspicions, she kept them to herself.

"Ralph's not going to be too happy if you go chasing off to the beach with the crew coming to start combining wheat."

"He's not going to be too happy if I can't locate Kim, either. Anyway, I'll be back by tomorrow if I have to go all the way to Myrtle Beach. I'm taking the truck. You'll need the car if Daddy has to go anywhere. Look after him for me, will you, Lib?"

"I always do, don't I?" the housekeeper said dryly.

"And if Jo calls—"

"She won't. Honey, she's fourteen years old, not four. Besides, I don't think they have phones in the girls' dorm at Camp Laurel Hill."

"Yes, but if she does, tell her... tell her I'll call her back the minute I get home, okay?"

Carrie raced for the stairs to shower and change, decided against it when she glanced at the clock, and took time only to grab her purse. "See you in the morning, if not before, and if Kim shows up, you sit on her until I get back, you hear me?"

She didn't want to think about what her father was going to say if Kim stayed out two nights in a row. Lib had let him think she was with a girlfriend, and Carrie hadn't told him any different, but they couldn't protect him from the truth much longer.

What if something was really wrong? What if Kim had run away? Where could she have gone? Honestly, sometimes Joanna at fourteen was more mature than Kimberly was at eighteen!

And at thirty, there were days when Carrie felt more like a hundred.

Two

It was three-twenty by the time Rex headed south on I-85. Hot and steamy, it was a great day to be headed for the beach. Not such a great day to be hightailing it south after a half-baked kid who wasn't going to thank him for horning in on his date.

Rex still hadn't taken time to eat since breakfast. He was tired, hungry and feeling raw after running head-on into a past he thought he'd put behind him. The fact that for once his high-tech methods had netted him precisely nothing had been a real blow, too. The top fraud investigator for the state justice department, with a passkey to more information than the average person knew existed, and he couldn't even get a line on his own kid brother!

But it had been seeing Carrie again that had knocked him out. It scared the hell out of him that she could still affect him the way she had all those years ago. He thought he'd outgrown her by now. God knows, he'd tried hard enough.

At sixteen, Rex had been no great prize. Sixteen was a bad time to learn that your parents weren't your parents. A few years younger and he could have stashed away the knowledge with his childhood and gone on from there. Maybe. A few years later and he might have been mature enough to handle it. Maybe. But sixteen is a hell of a time to find out that your real parents were a couple of kids who'd gotten into trouble, couldn't handle it and either died or ran away.

John and Elizabeth Ryder had desperately wanted a son. Instead, they'd had a daughter. Then Elizabeth had learned that she couldn't have another child, so they'd adopted an infant, named him John Rexford Ryder and settled in for the long haul. But then Elizabeth had died, and a few years later John had remarried, and his second wife had given him the son he'd always wanted.

Rex had long suspected that if John Ryder could have taken back his name and given it to his real son, he would have done it. But it was too late. Sensing his father's feelings, Rex had reacted by striking out at whatever targets presented themselves. As the bitterness grew inside him, he'd rebelled every way he knew how. God knows where he would have ended up if he hadn't met a tiny fireball named Carrie Lanier.

Everything about her had appealed to him, and to this day he couldn't say why. She wasn't the prettiest girl at Durham County High, nor the smartest one. Hell, he'd never even seen her in a dress! But they'd taken to each other right off, recognizing a kindred spirit. And perhaps a kindred need.

For the first time in his life, Rex had found a reason to look forward, instead of backward to a past he couldn't change. Carrie had been barely fifteen, and he'd been sixteen, all bravado and rampaging hormones, but they had laughed together. He'd told her more about himself, his dreams, and the demons that drove him, than he had ever told another soul, but once he'd learned how young she was, he had tried to keep his hands to himself. Tried and failed.

It had been in the spring of his senior year when they had finally succumbed to the overwhelming attraction that had sprung up between them. Two and a half months later, her father had found out and told his, and John Ryder had shipped him off to the other side of the country. Rex had tried to see Carrie and explain, but between his father and hers, there'd been no chance.

He had seen her at the graduation exercises. She had sat across the room with her family, eyes front and center, shoulders squared, hands lying still in her lap. That had told him more clearly than words how much she was hurting, because Carrie couldn't talk without her hands. It had been one of the things he'd teased her about.

He had made up his mind then and there that he was coming back for her. He would give her a few years, and then he was coming to claim her.

But first he had to show his father and hers—and maybe himself, most of all—that he could make it on his own. God, what a jackass he'd been!

But he had succeeded. Eventually. By the time he'd come back home to stay he had three degrees and four excellent job offers. He could have walked right up and cocked a fist under Ralph Lanier's nose, and he'd wanted to. Damned if he hadn't wanted to face down the man who had once called him a no-good bum who'd be lucky to get a job mucking out holding pens.

But by that time it had already been too late. While he'd been working his tail off at any job that had paid a buck and studying himself blind every night, Carrie had been getting herself married and starting a family. If he lived to be a hundred, he would never forget the way he'd felt that day in Fowler's parking lot, when he'd heard a child call her

Mama, Mama—heard someone else call her Mrs. Jennings.

The radials sang on the Interstate, a soothing background for Rex's turbulent thoughts. He told himself to forget about Carrie, to think about Billy. To figure out what he was going to say when he caught up with that young scamp.

What *could* he say? Billy was old enough to know what he was doing. These days kids learned the facts of life in kindergarten, and at twenty-one a guy didn't need permission to sleep with a woman.

Irrelevant, the rational part of his brain countered. An experienced woman was one thing, but that was a high school kid Billy was fooling around with. She might have turned eighteen, but they could still end up messing up both their lives if somebody didn't talk some sense into their heads. All the safe sex education in the world couldn't prevent the emotional trauma that could result from one careless moment.

Edging a few miles over the speed limit, Rex narrowed his eyes against the late-afternoon glare. The early June sun packed a mean wallop, and despite the brassy look to the sky, there wasn't a cloud in sight to promise relief.

Turning up the air conditioner, he continued to rack up arguments on both sides of the issue, SOP for a man who tracked down white-collar criminals using mainly a computer and his own powers of deduction.

If Billy was planning on impressing his girlfriend with a weekend at Stella's beach house, he was going to be pretty damned disgusted when big brother horned in on his little love nest. Was it worth the strain on their relationship? Maybe. Maybe not. On the other hand, the last thing any young lover needed was Ralph Lanier and his pitchfork brigade riding to the rescue.

On still another hand, this was the nineties. Society had changed. These days they handed out condoms in junior high school.

Whoopee.

Yeah, society had changed, all right, Rex thought tiredly. The trouble was, human nature hadn't. Guilt, rational or not, could still mess up an otherwise sound mind, and he didn't want Billy's head any more screwed up than it already was.

Feeling a lot older than his thirty-two years, Rex gave up trying to rationalize the situation and concentrated on driving. Just south of Kannapolis, the flow of traffic began to congeal. Five-twenty on a Friday afternoon in early June, with school just out for the summer, was enough to put a strain on the system under the best of conditions. And these were hardly the best of conditions. Up ahead, a double trailer had come unhitched, the rogue boxcar had creamed a Honda, and the resulting mess had cars backed up two miles.

While he waited, Rex placed a call to his office and another one to his hacker friend. Neither call produced results. Sweating and swearing, he inched forward. His shirt was stuck to his back, his stomach was pumping enough acid to dissolve Mount Rushmore and his head was pounding like a jackhammer from glare and tension.

This was definitely not the way he'd planned to spend his vacation! If it had been anyone but Billy—anyone but Carrie...

The mental image of a fiery-haired little bundle of dynamite in faded blue denim filled his mind, and he swore a mild oath. His stomach growled. Traffic ground to a standstill once more and he switched off the engine and rolled down a window, only to be treated to a blanket of dust-laden heat and a kidney-stone-shattering blast of hard rock music from the Trans-Am chafing at the bit in the next lane.

Dammit, he didn't need this. What he needed was a meal. And a shave. What he needed was to get his mind off Carrie.

"Oh, hell," he grumbled. "Somebody's got to prove that not all the Ryder men carry their brains below the belt!"

Right or wrong, he somehow felt responsible, and Rex knew he wasn't going to be satisfied until he'd checked it out. Which only added credence to the old saw about the wildest boys turning out to be the strictest parents. Or in this case, the strictest big brothers. And Rex had been wild, all right. Maybe not as wild as his reputation had painted him, but wild enough to know that if he could save Billy a few missteps along the way, he had to do it.

Once the wreckage was finally cleared away, traffic flowed evenly through Charlotte and then began to thin out. Rex was doing a steady seventy-four, headed toward the state line, when he spotted the red pickup truck pulled over in the emergency lane, the hood raised and a white rag tied to the door handle. He spared it the briefest glance as he whipped past.

And then he swore, scowled into his rearview mirror and swerved to the right. It was the sight of a pair of blue chambray shoulders topped by a mop of red hair that did it. One fleeting glimpse through a dusty windshield of a slumping figure and a bowed head was enough to make him slam on his brakes and shift into reverse.

She looked utterly defeated, and Rex felt a painful twist in his gut that had nothing to do with hunger. Carrie Lanier, down for the count? Oh, no. Not his little Carrie!

Carrie *Jennings*. He kept forgetting that.

By the time Rex had closed the distance between them, he told himself he must have been mistaken. She was out of the cab and leaning against a front fender, every inch of her small, voluptuous body, from the pointed toes of her dusty western boots to the stubborn thrust of her rounded chin, an unspoken challenge. Whatever tenderness Rex had felt at the sight of her slight form slumped over the steering wheel of a broken-down rust bucket evaporated the minute she lit into him.

"You might as well shove off. I don't need your help!"

"I didn't offer any." As a greeting, it lacked a certain warmth, but after the kind of day he was having, Rex was in no mood to be diplomatic. "Where the hell do you think you're going, anyway?"

"Where does it look like I'm going? I'm on my way to Myrtle Beach to rescue my sister before that rotten creep ruins her life!"

Feet planted firmly on the rough pavement, she crossed her arms over her generous breasts. Rex crossed his own. Dammit, she had no business barging back into his life and getting him all stirred up again! "Yeah. Sure. You do that. What motel does your sister usually use for this kind of thing?"

Ninety-nine pounds of dynamite exploded. "*What* kind of thing? Just what are you implying?"

"Precisely what you're inferring!" Rex struggled for control. Carrie was the one with the temper. He had never had a problem with his. At least not in the past ten years. "Look, I'm not implying anything," he said tiredly. "I only wanted to know where you're planning on looking. Myrtle Beach covers a lot of territory."

"That's not what you said!"

He wiped a trickle of sweat out of his eyes. "You want it in words of one syllable? I asked wh—"

A tractor trailer roared by, wind whipped over them, and Carrie clasped her hands over her ears. When she swayed in the after-blast, Rex actually found himself reaching out to steady her. Abruptly, he stepped back and dropped his hands. Dammit, he wasn't going to let her get to him. Not this time!

"Okay, so you think she's somewhere in Myrtle Beach," he said, his voice unnaturally calm. If he was going to be stuck with her again, he couldn't afford to forget the way she used to turn him on with her belligerence and then knock the props out from under him with her damned vulnerability. "I take it you've got a reason for thinking that?"

Carrie scowled. "Of course I— Well, no—that is, not exactly. But I have to start somewhere."

"Go on," he said grimly. The paved emergency lane was hot, noisy and probably dangerous, and all he could think about was what she had looked like naked from the waist up. Naked and needy under a cold March sky.

"Well, I certainly didn't come this far on a whim! For one thing, Kim's best friend, Allie Nuckles, said Kim bought a new bathing suit the other day. Kim's been begging me for months to give her and a friend a week at the beach as a birthday present. I thought she meant to take Allie," she whispered, her voice suddenly drooping.

Rex only half heard what she said. He could no more keep from staring at her than a bull could ignore a red flag waving under his nose. In the brassy gleam of the setting sun she looked radiant, but it was an illusion. All the fight had drained out of her. She was as tired, harassed and worried as he was. And dammit, he hated seeing her this way!

He almost wished she'd fire up again. Her anger he could handle. He wasn't at all sure he could deal with a needy, vulnerable Carrie Lanier. Where the devil was her husband? Why wasn't he looking after her? "So? What now?" he prompted gruffly. Fascinated, he watched the process as she pulled herself together.

Head up, chin out, shoulders braced, she said, "She'll be at the Mimosa Terrace. It's where we always used to stay when we went to the beach."

"And if you draw a blank?"

"Then I'll go through the phone book until I find her. I don't know what else to do."

Rex pictured the massive beach area phone book and decided to change the subject. "What happened to your truck?"

"The transmission." When Rex lifted his brows, she added, "At least that's what it felt like. Our mechanic said last month that the bands needed adjusting, but I haven't been able to spare it long enough to take it in."

"Have you sent for help?"

"REAC's sending a tow truck from Charlotte," she said tiredly, referring to the road emergency channel of the CB radio.

They were silent for several minutes, staring at the steady stream of late-day traffic. The noise made talking difficult, but neither of them suggested getting into one of the two vehicles.

Carrie couldn't remember a time when she'd felt as acutely aware of a man. Not in the past fifteen years, at least. In boots, tight jeans and a black T-shirt, with his skin bronzed from the sun, Rex had taken her breath away. Now, years older and dressed in an open-necked shirt, a pair of khakis and buckskin loafers, he should have looked like any ordinary businessman taking a few days off from the office.

He didn't. It was still there under a thin layer of civilization—that raw sensuality. The latent power. That certain element of danger lurking behind those cool gray eyes.

Carrie's gaze lifted to his mouth, and she stopped breathing. She closed her eyes for an instant, fighting a rush of memory, and when she opened them again, they lighted on his hands, and it was even worse.

Clearing her throat, she said, "So... what are you doing in South Carolina? I thought you only worked in North Carolina."

Oh, great. Now he'd think she'd been pumping Billy about him, and she hadn't. Not really. But with Billy seeing so much of Kim, it was only natural she'd hear a word now and then about Rex. Was that her fault?

Of course if anyone ever found out that her high school annual still fell open to the page with Rex's picture, she would purely shrivel up and die!

"I do," he replied, but by then Carrie had all but forgotten her own question. "I'm not working now. I thought I'd better see if I could round up Billy before he got in any deeper."

"You don't have to bother. I'll send him packing the minute I find them, you can bet on that." She dared another look at his face, and then she wished she hadn't. No man had a right to be that handsome! God should have made him a wimp or a jerk just to give women a fighting chance. Maybe if he spoke in a squeaky falsetto instead of those deep, lazy tones that vibrated along her spine like the bass notes of a pipe organ, it might have watered down the effect of his physical impact, but he didn't. Memories and photographs were bad enough. In the flesh, he was lethal!

"It's no bother. I thought I'd check out Stella's place at Hilton Head. I've called, but the phone's not in service."

"Because they're not there. I told you, Kim likes Myrtle."

"Billy prefers Hilton," Rex said flatly.

"He would," Carrie retorted. Sighting an approaching tow truck, she stepped to the edge of the emergency lane to flag it in.

Rex yanked her back. "What the hell do you think you're doing? It's not going to help matters if I have to waste time scraping you off the pavement!"

Carrie tried to jerk her arm free, but Rex's grip was like iron. She caught a whiff of a subtle cologne, blended with the scent of masculine sweat and freshly laundered cotton, and her knees turned to water. "Would you please let go of my arm! I didn't ask you to stop!" They were still glaring at each other when the tow truck operator swung out of his vehicle and looked over the situation.

"Trouble?" the man asked, shifting his toothpick as he spoke.

Carrie opened her mouth to respond to the obvious. Before she could utter a sound, Rex said, "Probably the transmission."

"If you *don't* mind!" She turned to the other man and said, "I think it's the transmission, but it might be something else. I had all the hoses and fan belts replaced last month." Carrie knew her way around under the hood of most things mechanical, in a basic sort of way. Managing a farm the size of her father's, a woman had to know something about everything that went on, and a lot of it was mechanical. She was in no mood to defer to anyone, but under the circumstances, she had little choice. While the two men checked inside the cab and under the hood, she tapped her foot in growing irritation.

Finally, the truck driver came back, wiping his hands on a filthy rag. "Okay, we're ready to roll. You ridin' wi' me, lady?"

"She's riding with me," Rex answered for her.

Carrie swung around, her mouth open to let fly a few choice remarks, when he added, "To the nearest car rental agency."

They were still standing beside Rex's car when her poor upended truck was hauled away. Carrie did a quick mental rundown on her resources. The tow charge would be added to the repair charges, which would probably be astronomical. That, added to the cost of renting a car for at least a day, would mean . . .

"Unless you'd rather team up," Rex offered.

"I'd rather not be here at all," Carrie snapped, to which he added a heartfelt amen. What the devil had he been thinking of? It was bad enough just seeing her again, knowing she probably hadn't even waited for him to leave town before she'd taken up with some other guy. It would have had to be pretty damned quick for her to have married and produced a kid by the time he'd come back for her five or six years later.

"Well?" she demanded.

"Let's go. If you need to call home, you can use my car phone."

Carrie allowed herself to be helped into the pale leather interior of the powerful, low-slung sports car. In her dirty work clothes, she felt like a dung beetle at a garden party. "No, thanks," she muttered. "Lib knows where I am."

Lib. That was the housekeeper, wasn't it? "She's still there? You're lucky. Stella can't keep a maid longer than a few months."

"Lib's more like family."

"What about your, uh—other family?"

She sent him a curious look. "What other family? You mean Daddy? Lib will tell him whatever she thinks he needs to know."

Dammit, he hadn't meant Ralph. He wanted to know about her husband! About her children. He did . . . and he didn't. And if that made him seven kinds of a fool, so be it. "I guess Lib takes care of your kids now, huh?"

"My what?"

"Children. Or child. It must be, what... about twelve, fourteen years old by now?" He couldn't remember if the child was a boy or a girl. It had been dressed in unisex denim overalls. The thought that she might have a daughter the age Carrie had been when he'd first known her slammed into him with the force of a rocket.

Carrie stared unblinkingly at a squashed bug on the windshield. He knows, she thought. Oh, God, he knows! "Did Billy tell you?"

"I saw you and your child in Fowler's parking lot one day about nine or ten years ago."

"Oh." Her mind worked furiously. Had he guessed? Even at four, Jo had looked so much like him that Carrie had often wondered why no one else seemed to notice.

Or maybe they had.

"Who did you marry, Carrie? Do I know him?"

Fortunately, the car tracked like a locomotive, because Rex was staring at her as intently as she was staring at that damned dead bug.

"No, he's—that is, Don worked for Daddy. You probably wouldn't have known him."

"Jennings, right? I heard someone call you Mrs. Jennings that day. Are you happy, Carrie? Is he good to you?"

"Don and I have been divorced for nearly seven years. I took back my own name." Don had begrudged her his in the end, but she saw no reason to tell him that. "And yes, I'm happy." Contented would be a better word. Resigned an even better one.

Rex gripped the steering wheel until his knuckles whitened. *Why?* Why had she married? Why had she divorced? Had she instigated the separation or had he? Was she still carrying a torch for the bastard?

A hundred questions logjammed in his throat, and Rex sought refuge in the mundane. "Look, it's nearly seven and I haven't eaten since breakfast. Unless you've got a serious objection, I'm going to hunt up the nearest restaurant and take a break." Which would give him a little time to think before he loused up the next fifteen years of his life!

"I'm not hungry. I think we should go on if we want to get there before it's too late."

"Carrie, it's already too late in the sense you mean."

Her hands flew up in exasperation. "Oh, so that's it! Since the cows are already out, why bother to shut the barn door, right?"

"Don't start with me, okay?"

But Carrie couldn't help herself. Outspoken at the best of times, her tongue ran away with her whenever she was nervous or worried. At the moment, she was both. "If you're not serious about going after them, you can let me out right here! I'd rather take my chances on hitching a ride than—"

"Carrie, I'm warning you." Rex down shifted with all the finesse of a beginning driving student and swore between clenched teeth. Swamped in unanswered questions, he was having enough trouble dealing with his libido without having to deal with her hotheaded independence.

Adjusting the A/C to a lower level, he thought about the sheen of perspiration on her tanned forehead when she'd first launched herself out of her truck back at the cabin.

And that was another thing, dammit! Redheads weren't supposed to tan, they were supposed to freckle! By now she should have filled out into a solid little butterball, with freckles, faded hair and half a dozen kids swinging on her skirts.

And it wouldn't have made a damned bit of difference, he knew to his sorrow. Because Carrie was Carrie, and she was special. Big or little, round or square, she got to him like no other woman in his not inconsiderable experience.

Seven years. He could have kicked himself in the rear when he thought of all the time he'd wasted! He almost wished she were still married. He wished she had three husbands and a dozen kids! Instead, she looked just the same. No, even better. There was a maturity about her now that honed her beauty right down to her elegant little bones. Something about the eyes. And the mouth...

The first time he'd ever seen her, he'd been struck by her rare combination of pride, innocence and temper wrapped up in a shapely little package. She'd been an irresistible challenge, and in those days, he'd thrived on challenges.

Still did. Only these days, his challenges involved brain work, computer skills and a lot of educated instincts instead of fast cars, fast girls and fistfights.

He sighed. Yesterday was gone, but if he played it right, he just might gain a toehold into the future. "So... how've you been otherwise, Carrie?" he ventured.

She eyed him warily. "Fine."

"The years don't seem to have done you any harm. You look great."

"Thank you." She sounded surprised. Rex decided not to push it. Time was on his side. If he took it one step at a time, maybe, just *maybe*...

A solid wall of slate-gray clouds had moved in over the pale yellow sky, making driving somewhat easier. Lulled by the steady hum of the tires, Carrie began to relax until a flash of lightning brought her up against her seat belt. "Tell me it's not going to rain," she wailed.

"It's not going to rain," Rex repeated dutifully. "On the other hand, it usually does. Eventually."

"But we're supposed to start combining wheat tomorrow. It *can't* rain!"

"Then it won't." Rex reached out and switched on the radio. The quadriphonic strains of Whitley's "I'm No Stranger to the Rain," filled the cozy interior, and their eyes met. Rex quirked a grin. Carrie grimaced.

"Hey, it's only a song," he told her, but then the song ended and the announcer came on with a weather update that had Carrie groaning and burying her face in her hands.

"A slow-moving front pushing severe thunderstorms has spawned tornadoes in Alabama and South Georgia, and is expected to be moving into our area within the next hour. There've been reports of flooded creeks and damaging hail in some areas. All interests in the area are advised to—"

"Which area?" Carrie demanded, but Rex shook his head. They listened through two dismal ballads and five minutes of commercials for a clue as to the origin of the broadcast, and finally Rex switched the radio off.

A spattering of rain struck the windshield. Carrie crossed her arms over her chest. "Great! Even if it doesn't mess up my combining, it's going to follow us all the way to Myrtle Beach."

"Sorry about your combining. If we head south instead of east, we'll probably miss the storm."

"Why bother? Kim's in Myrtle. You go to Hilton Head if you want to, but drop me off somewhere where I can rent a car first."

"Neither of us is going anywhere until we get something to eat. We'll talk about it after that."

Carrie crossed one leg over the other and then switched them around. She sighed hard and heavy. She crossed her arms over her chest and sighed some more until Rex had had all he could take. "Look, dammit, if they spent last night together, I don't see what the big rush is all about! It's not as though either one of them is a virgin, for cripes sake! Get real, Carrie!"

"I got real thirty years ago," she snapped back. "The only reason Mama married Daddy was that she got caught. With me! Don't think she ever let me forget it, either! She could have married the son of a bank president—of the president of the United States, for all I know! She sure as shooting didn't plan on being forced to marry some redneck dirt farmer!"

"So what's your point?"

"My *point*," she exclaimed, waving her hands wildly, "is that I don't want that for Kim! I want her to have choices." The choices neither Carrie nor her mother had had.

Rex muttered something vaguely profane. "She's got choices. Things aren't like they were for our parents' generation. Or even for ours. Remember I told you about my own mother? How she had me when she was just a kid herself?"

"And died," Carrie reminded him. As if he needed reminding.

"Okay, so what I'm trying to say is that Kim and Billy have more options than our folks did. Besides that, you take any ten kids these days and eight of them will tell you stories about their backgrounds that will curl your hair. Times have changed, honey."

"Not that much," Carrie muttered, but by then Rex was pulling into a hard-hat type café. Besides, what good did talking do? Now she was worried not only about Kim, but about Rex's putting two and two together and coming up with the right number. Jo had been born precisely eight and half months after he'd left town.

The restaurant was unprepossessing, at best, the food plain country with few frills. Rex opted for country-fried steak and Carrie filled her plate from the hot buffet, choosing cabbage, turnip greens, pinto beans and corn bread. If he'd picked out this place because he thought she might be uncomfortable in a fancier establishment, she didn't want to disappoint him. She was country, and she wasn't ashamed of it!

"I'm paying for my own food," she muttered as they passed down the line toward the cashier.

"Who's arguing?"

The table was scarred and none too clean. Carrie squared her plastic utensils and her glass of milk and reached for the pepper vinegar which, along with catsup, graced each table. She liberally doused everything on her plate except for the corn bread, and if she'd thought of it, she would have ordered buttermilk and crumbled her bread into that, which probably would be going a bit too far, as she didn't even like buttermilk. "We're wasting time," she muttered. "You should have stopped at a drive-through and we could have eaten on the road."

Rex glanced at a gold and stainless steel wristwatch that had probably cost more than her best purebred bull. "You worry too much."

She dug into her dinner, blinked away the tears at the fiery seasoning, and studiously avoided looking up. "Sorry," she snapped.

"Are you enjoying it?" he asked after several minutes.

"Thank you, it's excellent."

"The steak's great. You should have tried it. I'd have thought you of all people would eat beef."

"I raise it. That doesn't mean I have to eat it."

He shrugged, finished his own meal and suggested dessert. Before she could allow as how she wouldn't mind a slice of coconut pie if they had any, the storm broke. Rain beat against the windows, accompanied by a steady barrage of lightning. Thunder served as a counterpoint to the bluegrass music from an FM radio somewhere in the room.

"You know we're not going to get far in this, don't you?" he asked. He signaled a waitress and ordered lemon pie and coffee for them both without consulting her, and for once she didn't challenge him. Somewhere along the way she seemed to have run out of steam.

"We're at least five or six hours from Hilton Head. I don't know about you, but I've already had a pretty long day," he said.

"Myrtle's not—"

"It's not all that much closer."

"What are you suggesting, that we give up?"

"I'm suggesting that we be sensible and get a good night's sleep before we end up in a ditch somewhere. It's going to be completely dark in another ten minutes, even without the rain."

"I can drive if you're tired."

"Oh, yeah, sure you can. Only we've still got a few things to settle before we go any farther."

"Columbia. Let's just go as far as Columbia." It was the turning-off place, the point of decision. If she couldn't convince him to go on by the time they got to where Highway 20 cut over toward Florence and Myrtle Beach, she would just have to rent a car. Although how she was going to manage on the amount of cash she'd brought with her was anyone's guess. The Laniers had never believed in plastic. Farming was too uncertain, and Ralph Lanier had a horror of getting into debt and losing everything. "I just wish I had my own truck," she grumbled, and Rex knew a moment of sympathy. Being dependent on him must gall the hell out of her.

But then she blew it. "If we do end up stopping, I'm paying for my own room, is that clear? And first I need to stop at a drugstore."

"A *drugstore?*"

"For toothpaste! I'd planned on finding Kim and heading back home tonight."

As it happened, Rex's gear was still in the car. He'd never gotten around to unloading back at the cabin. "Borrow mine."

"All right, but that sister of mine is going to be in hock to me for the next ten years after this little episode," she vowed, and they both knew it was as good as a surrender.

She was a fighter, though. Rex would have to hand her that. But it just so happened that he was a fighter, too, and now that he knew she was no longer married, he had something to fight for.

"I'd still rather go on a while longer. Maybe we could stop at a pay phone and I could call the Mimosa Terrace?"

"Call from the car." Rex made her wait under the shelter while he unlocked the car. Even so, she was soaked almost to the skin by the time she climbed in beside him. Instead of slacking off, the rain continued to drum down. Traffic inched along cautiously, with more and more of it pulling off into the emergency lane to wait it out as windshields steamed up and a few lighter-weight cars began to hydroplane on the wet, oil-slick pavement.

"You want to try to put through a call?" Rex raised his voice so he could be heard over the din, and Carrie leaned toward him to hear what he'd said.

"I'd better wait until it lets up. I don't even know how to use one of these things." A CB radio was more her speed. If she'd had her truck, she could have put out a CQ and asked someone to patch her through to the Mimosa Terrace.

Rex drove as fast as he dared. The defroster was running constantly, but it was no match for the sweltering humidity. Carrie dug out a crumpled tissue and wiped a circle for each of them, but it steamed up again within minutes. When they nearly rear-ended an unlighted horse trailer, Rex began to swear. "That does it! You might not value your neck, but I damned well do mine. We're getting off at the next exit and finding a place to hole up in until this thing is over, and I don't want to hear one word out of you about Columbia or toothpaste or Myrtle Beach! Is that clear?"

It was more than clear. Although she'd have died before she admitted it, Carrie ached all over from straining to see through the driving rain. She had a headache from trying to make sense out of blurred reflections of moving light rushing at them out of the darkness, and besides that, her stomach was beginning to hurt.

That damned pepper vinegar! What on earth had made her drown everything on her plate in the stuff? She didn't even like it that much!

Blame it on the fact that he had never tried to get in touch with her in all these years, other than a single letter he said he'd written, but which she had never received. Blame it on the fact that she had wasted too much time gazing at his picture in the annual, reliving every moment they had spent together.

Blame it on the fact that she had a constant reminder of how young and foolish she had been, in the form of a wonderful, exasperating, lovable child who looked more like her father every day.

The truth was, Carrie had holes a mile wide in her defenses where Rex Ryder was concerned. Always had. Probably always would.

Three

The motel was small and on the seedy side, a relic of the age of tourist courts. Even so, it was practically full. Evidently, they weren't the only travelers who had opted to hole up until the weather improved. While Rex headed for the office, Carrie let her eyes close as she gave in to tiredness and an increasing headache.

Nervous tension. A crazy barometer. It always served her this way. A warm bath and a few hours of concentrated relaxation, and she'd be in top form again, ready to take up the chase.

She watched him approach. He was wet to the skin, but he didn't hurry. He had a lazy walk—a lazy, sexy, hip-switching stride that was totally unconscious. With his rumpled khakis and wet shirt plastered to the lean length of his hard body, he would have set her pulses to pounding at her temples even if they weren't already.

Carefully faded, carefully tattered jeans had been all the rage when they were in school. Rex had worn black ones. Close-fitting, brass-bradded jeans that owed nothing to any fashionable designer. He'd worn boots, not Nikes. Thick-soled, lace-up boots that couldn't by any stretch of the imagination be called smart. And with all that, there wasn't a girl in Durham County High who wouldn't have given a month's allowance just to rest her palm on the curve of his small, tight behind for two minutes.

Woman, you really are sick in the head!

"I don't suppose you'd care to share?" Rex climbed back into the car and tossed a big brass key onto the dashboard.

Carrie swallowed hard and tried to regulate her breathing. He hadn't meant it, of course, but suppose he had? What would she have done? "Don't forget I need to borrow your toothpaste." Was that breathless little squeak the same voice that could make itself heard over the roar of a John Deere 12A bagger-type combine?

"You want something to sleep in?"

"I wouldn't say no to a pajama top."

He shot her a grin that had her scrambling madly to remember who she was and what she was doing there. "What would you say no to?"

"More rain and one more pickled pepper. You don't happen to have any aspirin, do you?"

Rex pulled in before the last one of seven identical cabins and shut off the engine. Reaching across her, he opened the glove compartment and handed over a small flat tin. "Anything else? I could offer to massage your temples for you."

In the flickering green light from the neon sign, Carrie couldn't quite read his expression, which was probably a good thing. "No, thanks. Aspirin, toothpaste and a pajama top will do me just fine. What time shall we meet? Five? Four? I'm used to getting up at dawn's early crack.''

Instead of answering, Rex ducked out, hurried around and opened her door, and Carrie had no choice but to dash for the skimpy shelter over the entrance. He unlocked the door and swung it open, and Carrie found a light switch.

"I'm afraid it's pretty shabby. Nothing else closer than twenty-seven miles, according to the night clerk. I took his word for it."

"You don't have to apologize. At least it's dry." It was tasteless and barren, but perfectly adequate. Of course, it probably wasn't up to Ryder standards, but then, neither was she.

"Wait here and I'll get my bag."

"You're not—" she began, but he was gone. A moment later, he was back. Flinging his dark hair off his dripping face, he placed a battered leather overnight bag on the arms of the room's only chair and unsnapped the latch.

His back was to her, and Carrie feasted her eyes. It was quite a feast. For a few seconds she allowed her imagination to range free. What if there had been only one available cabin? What if they'd had to share? Would he have—?

Would she?

"No pajamas. Sorry." He tossed her a T-shirt. "This should do well enough. Hang your clothes over near the air conditioner and they'll probably be dry by morning."

No, she answered her own question. She wouldn't. Couldn't afford to. Having been left high and dry, not to mention newly pregnant, had been bad enough the first time. If it happened again, she wasn't sure she could handle it.

"I hope to God those kids aren't out in this mess," he muttered as he dug into his toilet case and came up with a tube of toothpaste. Her brand, she noticed. At least they still had something in common.

Rex shut his bag and waited, unwilling to leave. She was edgy as a snake on ice. Hell, so was he, for that matter. "I guess you could say the situation is fraught with possibilities," he observed.

Carrie looked down at her boots, which were no longer dusty but no less disreputable for all that. She looked at the bed and then quickly glanced away. Tension shimmered in the cramped space, and she shifted her weight from one foot to the other. Did she want him to stay? One word would do it.

"We never did make that call to the Mimosa place," he reminded her. "Want me to give it a try?"

"Terrace. Mimosa Terrace. I wish you would," she said and sighed. She was clutching his T-shirt in both hands like a shield, and Rex's imagination started brewing up a heady concoction of the two of them stranded for weeks in a small bedroom, with Carrie wearing his T-shirt and him wearing even less.

Turning away abruptly, he reached for the phone, asked for information and then dialed through.

"I'll pay for the call, naturally," Carrie said defensively. "And my room." He waved her to silence, but after a few more moments, she went on. "Although if your brother hadn't talked Kim into running away with him, none of this would have happened. What's the matter, can't you get through?"

"Evidently the night clerk's too busy to answer the phone, and I doubt if Billy had to talk very hard. My guess is Kim's just as much to blame as he is."

"You would stick up for him, wouldn't you? I suppose you think it's perfectly all right for a boy to seduce a girl and then talk her into running off for the weekend and worrying her family sick.''

"What makes you so certain Billy seduced her? It could just as easily be the other way around.''

Rex could tell by the sudden stricken look on her face that she was remembering the same thing he was remembering. He could have cut out his tongue. "Hello? Yeah, keep trying, will you?'' he said into the receiver.

"Kim's not like that!''

"Neither is Billy!'' Hell, he didn't know whether he was or not. He was male, though. And like most boys that age, he had a one-track mind where girls were concerned. "Anyway, your sister's old enough to know the score.'' He glared at her, told the operator he'd try again later and slammed the phone down. "Look, fighting isn't going to get us anywhere,'' he said tiredly.

"Fine! Who's fighting? I just want you to know that Kim's not wholly responsible for this mess. I know Billy, and I know you. Evidently, there's something in the Ryder genes, and that can be spelled either way!''

"Anybody ever tell you you've got a nasty mouth on you?'' What the hell was he doing, slinging insults when he'd rather sling her over his shoulder and tumble her onto that sagging double bed?

But for now, at least, insults were the safest course. One way or another, he was going to have her again, but when he did, it wouldn't be in any seedy, two-bit hole in the wall, when they were both too strung out to enjoy it to the fullest.

"Has Kim ever done this sort of thing before?''

"Of course not!''

"There's no of course about it. Eighteen-year-old girls these days do pretty much what they want to do, and—''

"I'm sure you're an expert on what eighteen-year-old girls do," she snapped, her hands silent for once as they braced her hips.

"If you'd let me finish, I was going to say, so do twenty-one-year-old guys."

Her hands flew off her hips and waved wildly in the air. "Oh, great! That's a real big comfort!"

The trouble was, they knew each other too well. There was too much history between them, some of it unbelievably wonderful, some of it too painful to bear.

She glared at a monstrous plaster lamp. Rex's eyes took on a rare twinkle. "Carrie?" he taunted softly. Even tired and irritable, he enjoyed teasing her. Enjoyed it entirely too much.

Carrie turned back to face him, and then wished she hadn't. His hair, black with rain, had fallen forward onto his forehead again, and with his wet clothes glued to his body, he reminded her far too much of the old Rex—the Rex who had claimed her heart, soul and body, and then tossed them carelessly aside.

"Come on now, honey, everything's going to look better in the morning. The sun's going to shine, we'll catch up with the kids and all our troubles will be over."

"Oh, what do you know about troubles, anyway?" Carrie grumbled, but she had to smile, all the same. Fetching Kim back home before Daddy blew a fuse was important, but it wasn't the end of the rainbow by any means. At least not for the Laniers.

Carrie knew a sudden crazy urge to curl up in Rex's arms and forget all about Kim, about weeks of drought when the corn was so dry it looked like a field of pineapples, about weeks of rain just when the wheat was ready to combine. About the falling price of beef and the rising price of everything else, and the danger of her father's having another accident in that confounded golf cart of his, and herself growing old with nothing more to show for it than a child who was already far too independent and a hard-scrabble farm that demanded all her time and energy, and gave nothing in return.

Why couldn't she steal a few hours for herself?

"Are you going to stand there in those wet clothes all night?" He was beside the door, bag in hand, and Carrie suddenly wondered if he had a wife. Or a fiancée—or at least a mistress. Men like Rex Ryder could have any woman they wanted, and she knew from personal experience that he was no monk. "Shouldn't you call your family to let them know where you are so they won't be worried?"

"Why bother? I'm not sure where I am, and I don't know where I'll be tomorrow." Unlike her, he didn't have any real family—leastways, none that really belonged to him. But then, she didn't know that, did she? Unless she'd asked Billy about him.

"What if your wife needs to get in touch?" she persisted.

Rex hid a quick burst of satisfaction. "Fishing Carrie? That's not like you."

Up went the chin, back went the head. Rex could practically hear her spine clicking into alignment. "You haven't the least idea of what's like me and what's not," she said stiffly. "If you'll excuse me, I'll go squirt out enough toothpaste for now and for in the morning, and give you back your tube."

Rex watched her march across the room toward the cramped bathroom. Women built the way Carrie Lanier was built had no business wearing jeans. He remembered telling her that fifteen years ago. That much, at least, hadn't changed.

She was back in a minute to hand him the Colgate, confident that she had her emotions under control. Of all the men in the world to be stranded with at a motel in the middle of a thunderstorm, why did it have to be the only man in the world she had ever begged to make love to her?

"Will you leave a wake-up call?" she asked, proud of the evenness of her voice.

"Wrist alarm. I'd trust it a hell of a lot more than I'd trust our night clerk. Five suit you?" And when she nodded, he said, "Five it is, then. G'night, Carrie."

Rex stood just outside the door for several moments, wondering if he wasn't carrying chivalry a bit too far. He needed a shower. He needed a bed, not a cramped back seat in a closed-up car. But if he'd told her there was only one room at the inn, and she'd insisted on sharing, there was no question in his mind how they'd end up.

And God, he wanted it! More than he'd wanted anything in years, he wanted to go back inside, sling his bag on her chair, kiss the living daylights out of her and then share her bath, her bed and her body... in that order.

Carrie dawdled in the tub, wondering if she should call his room and remind him of...

What? They'd said everything that needed saying. And a whole lot that didn't. Tomorrow she would have a better grip on herself. She'd better, because one thing was obvious—she was no more immune to him now than she had been fifteen years ago.

Damp, her skin pink and flushed from a deep, hot bath, she stood at the basin wearing Rex's T-shirt and a rubber band around her hair and brushed her teeth with a washcloth. It wasn't very satisfactory, but it would serve.

Irrelevantly, she recalled something she'd once heard about the test of true love being whether or not a girl would use her sweetheart's toothbrush. Did toothpaste count?

When the phone rang beside her bed, it took several moments for Carrie to recall where she was. Without opening her eyes, she grunted into the receiver.

"Are you awake?" Rex's early-morning voice was deep and husky.

"Course I'm 'wake!"

"Are you always this sweet first thing in the morning?"

"No, I'm usually vicious!"

"Thanks for the warning. May I use your bathroom?"

"Use your own." She yawned, stretched and rubbed her stomach, which seemed to have recovered from last night's assault by the pepper vinegar. She was hungry. "I'm starved. How soon can we leave and go find breakfast?"

"As soon as I find a place to shower and shave."

"What's wrong with your bathroom?"

"I don't have one."

She sat up, yawned again, and Rex said, "Carrie? Let me in."

"Rex, I don't—" But he was gone.

A moment later, Rex rattled the knob on her door. Every bone in his body ached, and he felt old and cranky and disheveled. When the door swung open, he nearly fell inside.

"I'd like to know what the devil you—"

"Later." Tossing his bag onto her rumpled bed, he strode across the room to the bathroom, last night's chivalry feeling more like damnfool idiocy in the cold light of day. It wasn't as if they were strangers.

Carrie was dressed by the time he emerged, except for her boots. Unlike most women Rex knew, she didn't use cosmetics. It occurred to him that with her coloring, makeup would have been gilding the lily.

"Would you care to explain?" she asked, her arms crossed over her ample bosom.

"What's to explain? There was one room available, the seats of my car are probably a hell of a lot better than that mattress over there, but not even the 850-i comes equipped with bathroom facilities. You ready to ride?"

Carrie's soft pink mouth fell open, and for one irrational moment, Rex was tempted to take advantage of it. But then, they'd be here all day, and he'd settled that matter in his own mind last night.

"Do you mean to tell me you—"

"Are you hungry?"

"Yes, but—"

"Then let's get moving."

They got moving. Nor would Rex stop long enough for her to settle her account at the office. "Already taken care of," he told her. One look at his set features and she had better sense than to argue.

"I called Stella again this morning." The sun was just creeping over the horizon. "Got the machine. Either she was out all night or she's a heavy sleeper. If Billy was there, he'd probably have caught it."

"Oh."

"Hey, are you all right down there?" Her socks had been damp, and rather than shove bare feet into wet boots, she had padded out barefooted. Now, thinking about a restaurant smelling of coffee and bacon and fresh hot biscuits, she was struggling to pull them on in the car.

"Shoes and shirts required," she grunted, jamming her left heel onto the inner sole of her boot. And when he still looked puzzled, she said, "Restaurants. You know, they always have a sign about shoes and shirts."

"I thought it was coats and ties."

"It probably is in your kind of restaurant. Mine aren't so picky." She tugged on the other boot and sat back, her face flushed from exertion, and Rex grinned appreciatively.

"Honey, you can eat in my restaurant any day, minus tie, coat, minus shirt, minus—"

"Thanks," she snapped, but she chuckled softly, and Rex settled back and concentrated on finding her the kind of breakfast he thought she'd enjoy. If he remembered correctly—and where Carrie was concerned, he generally did—it would be country cooking. No croissants, no Danish. Ham, grits, hash browns, biscuits and eggs.

"So how come you never put on weight?" he asked after several minutes had passed in surprisingly comfortable silence.

"Too busy. You try running a three-hundred-forty-acre farm shorthanded and see how far you get."

"Why shorthanded?"

She explained the difficulties of finding reliable help, the dangers of making do with unreliable help, and skipped over the difficulty of meeting a monthly payroll of even the most meager proportions now that beef was considered politically incorrect.

"Couldn't your father had hired himself a manager?"

"He did. I married him. He quit when we separated, end of story." Carrie tried to recall how much she'd told Rex about her home life all those years ago. That her father was a bitter man? She probably hadn't realized it herself back then. She'd only known that he was harsh and not given to smiling. Since then she'd come to realize that his bitterness had begun about the time he realized that his wife despised him, hated the farm and had no intention of being tied down with children.

Polly Lanier ran away when Carrie was eight and came back long enough to get pregnant with Kim. When Kim was a baby, she'd run off again, for the last time. Shortly after that, Ralph had hired Lib Swanson, and within a year, he'd rolled a tractor and crushed his legs.

"We get along all right," she summed up, but Rex could fill in the gaps. She worked her butt off for that hard-bitten, ungrateful sonovabitch, trying to make up to him for being a daughter instead of a son. Rex knew all about fathers who wanted sons.

He swerved into the parking lot of something called Mom's Kitchen. If Mom made decent coffee, she would have his undying gratitude.

Mom made decent coffee, crisp bacon, light-as-a-feather biscuits and scrambled eggs that didn't leak yellow water all over the plate.

Carrie insisted on paying her own tab, and Rex didn't argue. She'd always had the devil's own pride. He'd had a sneaking suspicion on more than a few occasions that it was just about all she did have. She'd never had much in the way of pretty clothes, no allowance for burgers or records or sodas between classes. But pride she had never lacked.

When they got back to the car, Rex tried the Mimosa Terrace again. This time the call was answered. He ran down the list of possibles—Kim Lanier, Billy Ryder, Mr. and Mrs. W. Ryder. There wasn't even a John Smith registered.

"What next?" he asked. He could tell that Carrie was pretty discouraged. She'd counted on winding this thing up today and getting back home. Hell, so had he for that matter, although the outcome was beginning to matter less and less to him.

"Could you try your place at Hilton Head again?" she asked meekly.

He had tried it last thing the night before and first thing this morning, but he tried again. With the same results.

"That doesn't necessarily mean nobody's there," Carrie said.

"It doesn't mean they are, either."

"No." Her hands rested on the thighs of her still-damp jeans, and she sighed heavily.

"You know you don't need to sit around all day in wet clothes," Rex said gently.

"I'll dry out eventually. Denim takes forever."

"Did you hang your things by the A/C like I told you?"

"It conked out sometime during the night. I should've reported it."

"Forget it. How's the head this morning?"

"Better, thanks. How do you feel after being cramped up in the back seat all night? Rex, I feel so guilty about that."

They hit the Interstate and sped south. "No need. I've slept in a lot rougher places than that."

He thought for a minute she was going to ask about those places—almost wished she would. Just because he could afford to indulge himself with a few luxuries now, that didn't mean he'd come by any of them the easy way. Oddly enough, he found himself wanting to tell her about the job as a roughneck on an oil crew, with a logging team, as a bartender in a waterfront dump in Galveston, as a linesman with a small power company, where he'd blistered his hide and damn near lost his manhood skinning down a pole.

"At least the sun's shining," she said after a while, and when he reached for his sunglasses and winced at the protesting muscles in his arm, she apologized again for his uncomfortable night.

"Forget it," he said, jamming the glasses on his face.

"If you're going to moan and groan all day, I can't, can I?"

"Lady, if the time ever comes when my moaning and groaning get to be a problem, you can take the car and I'll walk, okay?"

He hadn't meant to snap, but dammit, she'd dug a bottle of hand lotion out of her purse and was slathering it all over her hands and arms, and even her face and her neck. It smelled like flowers—it smelled like woman, and that was the last thing he needed at this point!

"Sorry," she murmured.

"No, I'm sorry. I'll work the kinks out before long."

"A hot bath instead of a quick shower would've helped."

A cold shower would have helped even more, but he didn't bother to tell her that. She was hardly in a mood to appreciate it.

Dammit, why did it have to be Carrie? What was there about this one woman that made her linger in the backwaters of his mind all these years? It wasn't as if he'd never known another female. Hell, he'd known hundreds of women. Dozens, at least. Beautiful women. Successful ones, smart ones, sexy ones, wealthy ones—you name the category and he'd probably sampled it.

So why Carrie? Why not Maddie, who was an attractive, intelligent realtor with whom he'd enjoyed an intimate relationship for nearly a year now? Granted, he was inclined to drag his feet, mainly because his sister kept trying to shove the two of them toward the altar.

Before Maddie there had been Carol, who was a junior partner in a big law firm. And Macy, a captain with a small feeder airline. He could name a dozen women right off the top of his head with whom he might have fallen in love, married, and led a reasonably happy life.

But he hadn't. In spite of all the other women he'd known with varying levels of intimacy, there had always been Carrie, lurking in the back of his mind like a half-remembered dream.

When a dozen or so miles sped past with no comments, Rex glanced across the console. She was toying with a thread from a buttonhole on her shirt. "Worried?" he asked sympathetically.

"I just wish she hadn't run away. I mean, even if she is sleeping with him, if she'd talked to me, I could have advised her, and . . ."

His mouth clamped shut at that. He didn't need to be reminded that she would have gained most of her knowledge at the hands of some other man. His voice came out rougher than he'd intended when he said, "What could you have told her that would've changed one damned thing?"

Still toying with the thread, she said, "She's so young. Lib says she's spoiled and I suppose she is, but that's hardly Kim's fault."

"Yeah. Billy, too. He could've used a man's influence growing up. Stella's no great shakes as a mother."

The tires sang on the drying pavement. Rex studied the sky through the dark lenses of his glasses, noting the absence of clouds, uneasy, though, over the liverish color.

"I just hope we find them before it's too late."

"What would you consider too late?" he asked with a wry smile. "When you get right down to it, chasing after a pair of kids who've obviously been sleeping together, and who're both of legal age doesn't make a whole lot of sense."

"Do you want to turn back?"

"Do you?" he countered.

"I can't, but that doesn't mean you have to go on, if you'd rather not. I can go the police, I suppose."

"Which police? North or South Carolina? And what are you going to report? That a twenty-one-year-old man and an eighteen-year-old woman have gone off together without asking your permission?''

''When you put it that way, it sounds silly, I know.'' She gave up on the thread and started twisting the button. It was on the front of her shirt. If it came off, Rex wasn't going to be responsible for what happened next. A man could handle only so much temptation and stay sane, and Carrie Lanier, even in rumpled denims that smelled like a cattle barn, threatened to overload his circuits.

''Look, we both want to find out what's going on and I happen to be qualified to do the job. I guess we're stuck with each other for the duration.''

Four

When the silence between them had gone on too long, Rex switched on the radio again to hear a weather report that was basically a clone of the one they'd heard the day before.

"Damn," he muttered.

"Oh, no," Carrie wailed softy.

"Maybe we'll be out from under it before it gets too bad. Sounds like it's cutting across the northern part of the state."

"And the southern part of North Carolina," Carrie added. "If we can't get the wheat cut by Tuesday, the crew will have to skip us and go on to Mulvey's."

"You don't do your own combining?"

"It wouldn't pay us to own such a big piece of equipment. We share with three other small farms in the area."

They talked desultorily for a while about farming and when they fell silent again, Rex had a far better idea of just

what he was up against. The farm was a borderline operation. Ralph Lanier thought more of it than he did either of
his daughters. He could no longer manage alone and
couldn't afford to hire another manager. And Carrie had
been far too loyal to leave him for a life of her own.

"Talk to me," he urged a while later. "I need something
to keep me alert."

"You didn't get enough sleep last night," Carrie said
guiltily.

"Talk about something else. What have you plans for the
future, for instance?"

"The future?" she asked, as if the concept were a new
one. "Do you mean after we find the children?"

Rex had to laugh. "Do you have any idea how old we
sound, talking about the kids, the children? They're adults,
Carrie. Which makes us..."

"Super adults?"

"Hmm, I like the sound of that. As a super adult, if you
could have anything in the world you wanted, what would
you ask for?"

You. For the rest of my life, you, she said silently. "An
ice-cold cola in a bottle and a bag of salted peanuts."

"That's easy." A mile farther, he swerved into a rest stop.
When she came out of the ladies' room, he was waiting with
her refreshments, and she laughed and shook her head in
disbelief.

"What's the matter?" he asked as they sauntered back to
the car, Rex's arm slung carelessly across her shoulder.
"Didn't you believe me all those years ago when I told you
I could give you all the world's riches if you waited a few
years?"

"That must have been some other girl. You never promised me anything but to let me drive your Jeep, and you
never even did that." Carrie remembered too much for her

own peace of mind, but a promise of riches she definitely did not recall. Nor a promise that one day he would come back for her.

"You just weren't paying attention," he teased. "Too busy pouring peanuts into your drink."

But she did remember one promise that he hadn't kept. "You told me once you were going to take me to the beach one day and teach me how to bodysurf. I'll bet you didn't even know how yourself."

"I was planning it for your graduation gift," he claimed, and she snorted her opinion of that whopper.

"Well, how was I to know I'd be stuck in traffic in downtown Eugene the day you graduated? You didn't send me an invitation."

"I didn't know where you were, remember? Would you have come?"

He was silent so long she thought he'd forgotten the question. "Yeah, I just might have, Carrie Lanier. Of course, your old man would have held me off at the county line with a pitchfork, but I'd have given it a good try."

"Daddy's not like that," she declared, but not very convincingly. He'd always been overprotective of his daughters, even if he never spared them any affection. He loved Jo, though. If he loved anyone at all, it was his granddaughter. "How much farther is it?" she asked for the third time as they pulled out into traffic again.

"At a guess—three hours."

"Three hours!"

"Honey, time's not important. The important thing is finding that pair and making sure they're all right."

Carrie took a deep breath, staring straight ahead, and told herself that he was right, of course. Kim and Billy had been gone for two nights already. As long as they were safe, she supposed she should be happy. "All the same," she said aloud, "it was a thoughtless thing for them to have done. I don't have time to go chasing all over the country." She ripped open the plastic sack and jammed her cola between her knees so she could pour the peanuts into the bottle.

"It's hardly my idea of the perfect vacation, either."

Flinging her hair back over her shoulder, she glared at him. "Well, I certainly didn't invite you to come with me!"

"No, Miss Independence, you were stranded on the side of the road with a broken-down truck! If I hadn't happened to see you there and stopped—"

"I never asked you to stop!"

"I never said you did! Damned if I'm not beginning to regret picking you up off the side of the road!"

Carrie's mouth fell open. Her drink bottle tipped over. Fizzy brown liquid spread over one thigh and dripped onto the pale gray carpet. "Then why don't you just pull over right now and put me out?" she said very quietly.

Gripping the steering wheel, Rex pressed his back against the orthopedically correct seat back and breathed deeply. What the devil was he doing, picking a fight this way? "Carrie, I'm sorry. You know I didn't mean that." He couldn't blame it on the fact that she brought out the worst in him, because she'd always brought out the best in him. It was one of the inexplicable things about their relationship. Come to think of it, he didn't know too many women he'd have sacrificed a decent night's sleep for.

"I think maybe you'd better start yelling at me again," she said so meekly he did a double take. And then followed her gaze to the wet stain in her lap

"Oh, hell, honey, did I cause that?"

"Believe me, I'd be happy to let you take the blame. If my conscience would allow it. I really thought I had enough coordination to pour peanuts and quarrel at the same time."

"You're slipping." He grinned.

"You might not feel like laughing when you see the condition of your carpet."

"Hell, the ashtrays are full, anyway. Time to trade it in." He held out his hand and she poured peanuts into his palm, the way she used to do a long time ago. They'd always eaten a few first and then poured the rest into their drinks, something Carrie hadn't done in years.

Being together again brought back more than old memories, she thought ruefully. "Now I'm not only sticky, I'm salty, too."

"We'll stop at the next rest area."

"Which will be hours away."

"Maybe it'll rain. From the looks of those jeans, you could use a good shower."

"Bite your tongue," she said, smiling in spite of herself.

"I'd rather bite yours," he told her, and she subsided, feeling something lurch painfully in the vicinity of her heart.

For the next hour, they alternated between quick verbal duels, shared laughter and dangerously escalating awareness. Rex told himself he could have dealt with the situation with a lot more grace if he'd been prepared. But when a woman exploded into a man's life again after nearly half a lifetime—a woman he'd once loved with all the blind idealism of his misspent youth—then he could hardly be blamed for losing his grip, could he?

"Would you like for me to drive awhile? You keep hunching your shoulders as if your back hurts."

"It's getting even for the way I treated it last night. Thanks, honey, but no thanks. I've seen the way you drive, remember? You took out half an acre of landscape yesterday just getting that rust-bucket of yours off my property."

"Landscape? You mean that weed patch in front of your shack? I thought it was part of the county landfill, and I was trying to compact it for you." In spite of her soggy, sticky pants, Carrie felt her spirits rise. This was almost like old times. Teasing, trading taunts, secure in the knowledge that neither one of them would ever willingly hurt the other. If only...

"I remember another time I took you out there to that same place. You weren't all that critical of my landscaping back then."

She shot him a stricken look, and Rex swore under his breath. "Oh, hell, Carrie, I'm sorry. I guess I'm just not much of a morning person."

It was such a ludicrous misstatement that they both began to laugh. "What's your excuse the rest of the time?" she asked, but a smile hovered on her lips, and Rex took the out she offered.

"I'll plead the Fifth."

They were both silent after that. Traffic was surprisingly light, which helped, but the sky was growing increasingly threatening, which didn't.

Rex wondered about her sister. Was all this concern really warranted? Premarital sex was practically a given these days. Virgins, male *or* female, were an endangered, if not an extinct, species.

Was Carrie still blaming him for leaving without having said goodbye? It was hardly likely. She probably realized as soon as she'd had time to think about it that he'd done her a favor by taking off without pinning her down to any promises. She obviously hadn't wasted much time getting on with her life after he'd left.

As the heavy black car paced the flow of traffic on the Interstate, Rex set the speed and allowed his mind to range back in time. March had started out cold that year and then warmed abruptly. Brilliant blue skies had shone down on newly greening hardwoods, splashes of early yellow flowers, and the few traces of snow that remained under the laurel bushes on the north-facing bank of the river. The Eno along that particular stretch was not so deep as it was swift. There were a few hidden holes, but for the most part it was rocky.

On that particular afternoon Rex had been hunkered down on the tract of land John Ryder had promised to give him if he made it through high school. At that point, there'd been some doubt. His grades were marginal at best, because he didn't bother to apply himself. Still bitter over the discovery that the couple he'd thought were his parents were not, he'd been brooding about the awful possibilities of his biological heritage. Genetic engineering had been a relatively new concept back then, and he'd had too much imagination for his own good.

Lost in his own thoughts, he had caught a flash of red on the opposite bank from the corner of his eye, and stood up for a better look. It had been Carrie. He'd been vaguely aware that her father's farm was somewhere in the area, but he'd never known the exact location in relationship to the Ryder tract on the opposite side of the river.

He hadn't particularly wanted his privacy invaded that day, even by Carrie. Remaining perfectly still, he had watched her bend over a patch of yellow flowers and then get down on her hands and knees to pluck a few. And then something had caught her eye halfway down the steep bank—the same patch of purple, probably, that he could see from his own vantage point. He remembered calling out a warning to stay back, that the bank was crumbly from being frozen, but by then it was too late. She'd already begun to slide.

Arms flung wide, she'd struck at an angle and gone under immediately. Before she even surfaced, Rex had thrown off his sheepskin-lined jacket and raced down the opposite bank to plunge into the freezing water. She came up swearing before he was halfway across. Picking his way over the half-submerged rocks, he yelled to her. Startled, she turned, lost her balance and went under again.

By the time he got her ashore, they were both soaked to the skin. To this day, Rex didn't know why he'd carried her over to his side of the river instead of her own, but he had. His coat had been lying there where he'd flung it, and he'd snatched it up and carried her to a sheltered place where the cutting wind didn't reach.

Without bothering to ask, he began peeling off her layers. Tossing aside her sodden red coat and flannel shirt, he wrapped her in his coat, not bothering to slide her arms into the sleeves.

"You g-g-got all wet, too." She was shivering so hard she could barely catch her breath.

"Hey, hey now, stop shaking, baby," he murmured, rocking her in his arms. "You're going to start a landslide." It was steep, but not that steep.

"T-t-take back your co-co-coat, Rex. I'm all right n-n-now."

Busy checking her head for lumps or abrasions, Rex hardly felt the cold. He was soaked from the waist down, splattered from there on up, but he never even noticed. "You bump anything while you were down there? That's not exactly a swimming hole where you went down, short stuff."

Her lips were turning blue, and he opened the coat and brought her up against his body. For warmth, he tried to tell himself. Strictly for body heat. He carefully avoided looking directly at her chest, but he was aware of it. God, was he ever! Her full soft breasts in the heavy cotton bra were poking into his stomach, while her head was tucked up under his chin, and she looked so small, so scared and so very vulnerable, that Rex melted.

The first time he'd ever laid eyes on her he'd started figuring out how to get into her pants. It was a subject that had been on his mind a lot in those days—getting into girls' pants. Then he'd found out she was only fourteen and reluctantly, he'd postponed his plans and surprised himself by becoming her friend instead.

Naturally, he'd considered it his duty to straighten out any of the other guys who happened to get the wrong idea about her, and more than a few of them had, thanks to her overdeveloped little body.

They had talked a lot that first year, and he had come to appreciate her grittiness and her oddball sense of humor. The first thing that had struck him about her—after her breasts, at least—was that she wasn't put off by his reputation, which was pretty bad. That was one of the reasons that he'd always had a soft spot for her. Another was that she had never come on to him like most of the other girls, including some a couple of years younger than she was. Amazingly enough, she had seemed to trust him right from the first. Trust, he had soon come to realize, could be a real bitch of a burden.

"R-Rex, my f-f-feet are like p-p-popsicles!" she had told him.

"Hey, popsicles are my favorite frozen food!" Laying her down on a deep bed of leaves, he pulled off her boots, one at a time, and dumped the water out, noticing the paper-thin soles and the broken stitching. " 'Fraid these things have just about had it, honey."

"Daddy's going to kill me. They're only three years old."

"Never mind, we'll dry 'em out," he promised, and he'd lifted her small feet to warm them with his breath.

Looking back, he figured that it was just about then that his sense of self-preservation began to screw up. Instead of warming her feet the way he'd intended, he drew a pale toe into his mouth and suckled slowly, his eyes never leaving her face.

Carrie gasped and fell back onto her elbows, staring at him. The coat he had wrapped her in fell open, revealing a milk-white expanse of flesh above her belt, and Rex's rampant hormones leaped in response. Somehow he found himself lying on the ground, his legs tangled with hers and his arms sliding inside the fur-lined coat.

That was the beginning. At seventeen, Rex hadn't quite gained the upper hand over his sexual responses. As for good judgment, his had long since proven too erratic to be reliable. He knew damned well that it was mostly his wild reputation that appealed to girls—and some of them were no longer girls, but women. He traded on it shamelessly. At seventeen, he was experienced far beyond his years, his body's demands accustomed to being met.

This was Carrie, he reminded himself, but that no longer seemed relevant. She edged her face away from his throat, began to speak and then fell silent. They stared at each other, his gray eyes burning like dry ice into her wide brown ones. Mutely, she tilted her face to his.

One kiss, Rex promised himself. That's all he would take from her. Hell, he had to do something to get her circulation going again, didn't he? A shot of brandy would've done it, but the best he could do was beer, and that was up on the ridge in the Jeep. At least, he rationalized, a little cuddling would keep her from freezing.

Her mouth was incredibly sweet. Soft, moist and trembling under his. Somewhere in the back of his brains, he recognized her innocence, but it was already too late. His brain had relinquished control of his groin. At the first taste of his tongue, she stiffened in his arms. "Don't be nervous, Carrie—you'll like it. Open your mouth for me and I'll show you how to do it." He rolled over so that he was lying on top of her, bracing himself to spare her his weight.

"I don't know if we should be doing this," Carrie protested breathlessly.

"Why not? You don't want to catch pneumonia, do you?"

"I'm not all that cold anymore."

"Neither am I, baby, neither am I!" he whispered, unable to keep himself from grinding his hard pelvis against her softness. He lifted himself until her breasts were no longer flattened against his chest and gazed down. Wet, the white cotton contraption she was wearing was revealing enough that he could see the dark tint of her nipples, the turgid little peaks raised against the clinging cup.

"Your skin looks just like whipped cream," he told her, his voice rough and his hands unsteady. She was a temptation he could no longer resist. Slipping his hand beneath her, he quickly manipulated the hooks and eyes. At that age, he'd prided himself on his finesse, but when he slung the bra aside and gazed down at her ripe breasts with their pink, cold-stiffened tips, he just about lost it.

He swallowed hard, unable to speak. Up until then he had fancied himself an expert on women, but not even his agile seventeen-year-old imagination could have envisioned such lush perfection on such a miniature frame.

He must have said something, because she sat up, leaving his coat on the ground like a discarded cocoon, and crossed her arms in front of her. "Stop staring," she muttered.

Still bemused, Rex retrieved his coat and draped it over her shoulders again. "Carrie? What's wrong, sugar? You're not embarrassed, are you? They're great. They're, uh... magnificent." It wasn't a word he used very often—at least not about women. His rebuilt Triumph Spitfire was magnificent. The set of mag wheels he was saving up to buy were magnificent, but that was different. Carrie was different.

He touched her. She shuddered, her eyes big as chestnuts. She ducked her head, and Rex resisted the urge to reach out and touch her again. He wanted desperately to hurry her toward the ultimate goal, but he couldn't afford to frighten her.

"They're too big," she whispered. "Everybody makes fun of me at school. Maybe if I got real fat, nobody would notice, but no matter how much I eat, I never gain an ounce." Her face was flaming. When he sat back, she drew up her knees and lapped her right foot shyly over her left, staring at the mud stain on her knee.

"Geez, sweetheart, you don't have to be embarrassed just because you're st—I mean, you've got big, uh—chests."

"Everybody thinks I'm dumb, like I got these instead of brains. I hate it, I truly do! I'd rather be built like an ironing board. Nobody teases LouAnne Erwin because she's flat."

"You mean old two-bits? Sure they do, honey. I've heard she wears Band-Aids instead of a bra, didn't you hear that?"

A dimple flickered in her cheek, and Rex saw her lips tremble on the edge of laughter. She reached for her discarded bra, and he moved it out of her way. "Uh-uh. Better get the rest of those wet clothes off if you don't want to catch cold."

Smooth. Oh, he was so damned smooth. It was called technique, and Rex had used it shamelessly on more than one occasion to get what he wanted.

"I'd better get home and change before someone comes to find me. I was helping Odyous chase down the last of the strays. He's probably wondering where I am by now."

"Nobody's wondering anything. You haven't been gone that long, and anyway, they can't see us here for that bunch of bushes."

She tried to hold his coat together, but Rex, kneeling in front of her, refused to allow her to hide herself. He was about to burst out of his jeans at that point. There had to be somewhere more private he could take her! Those old mountain laurels weren't all that thick.

"The Jeep's parked up on the ridge," he said, impatient, but not wanting to risk being interrupted by some nosy farm type. "There's a blanket in the back."

Carrie kept casting nervous looks at the river. "My boots—Rex, where's my shirt?" She sat up then, and his coat slipped off one shoulder. The sight of her wet jeans outlining the soft feminine swell at the joint of her thighs piled coals on the fire in his loins. The pink nubs of her lush breasts poking out between her crossed arms blew on the flames, and the belt around her tiny waist, half-unbuckled where his clever fingers had already been at work, did the rest.

Eyes glazed, Rex launched himself at her, carrying her back down to the ground. He kissed her hard and long and deep, and after the first few moments she began to kiss him back, timidly at first, and then more eagerly.

By that time, he was nearly out of his mind. Gasping for breath, he lifted his head to stare down at her, and then he began to kiss her breasts, to suckle them until she was squirming on the hard, rocky ground. He'd managed to unfasten her belt and now the front zipper of her jeans was undone, and his hand was inside, fumbling clumsy caresses over her heated flesh.

He was so near the edge that he wasn't sure if he could get his own zipper down in time.

She gasped as he found his target. He felt a deep shudder go through her, and desperately, he began to count backward from ten. He would die of shame if he lost control the first time with her!

Oh, God, protection. It was the last thing on his mind, but this was Carrie.... She probably wasn't on anything yet.

It was in his wallet. The trick was to get it out and get it on before she could cool off. She wanted him, all right—he could tell by the way she was panting, by the way her hands were moving over his shoulders, in his hair, the way her fingernails were digging into his hips. She was wet and hot and ready.

"Just a minute, baby," he panted. "Let me get something out of my pocket."

"What?" Her breasts trembled with every beat of her heart, and he couldn't take his eyes off them.

"You know," he muttered. "Protection."

"Protection against what?"

Drawing back, Rex stared down at her. Was she kidding? No one was all that innocent.

"Snakebite," he snapped, furious with her for allowing him time to think. Dammit, he didn't want to think, he wanted to get on with it! He was hard and aching, and she was lying there, asking for it.

Well...maybe not asking for it, but she'd kissed him back, and she'd let him see her breasts—let him kiss them. Let him touch her between her legs, and she'd been damp.

The chill of suspicion set in. "Carrie, you have done this before, haven't you?"

"Done what before?"

"You know!"

"Made out with a boy?"

"Ah—" He uttered a four-letter word that shouldn't have made a farm girl flinch, but it did, and then he was embarrassed. Angry, frustrated and embarrassed, because he'd considered himself an expert when it came to sex. He knew he was good—he was smooth—and the girls he went out with were experienced enough to appreciate that fact. They always came back for more, didn't they?

So what the hell was he doing rolling in the dirt with a big-eyed little kid who didn't even know the score?

"You haven't, have you?" he said disgustedly.

"Sure I have," she snapped. She was sitting up by now, her arms crossed over her bosom once more, and her knees drawn up to hide her open zipper. "Lots of times. I know what you're talking about, I just—I forgot for a minute, that's all."

Picking up a stick, he jabbed it into the ground, not looking at her. "Come on, you've never done it before, have you?"

"I told you—"

"I don't mean fooling around, I mean *it*. Sex. Have you ever had sex with a boy?" He shot a glance at her and then looked away.

Dammit, she looked like she was about to cry! What did she have to cry about? He was the one who was about to explode!

"Not yet, but I've been meaning to. Honestly. Practically all the girls I know—"

"I'm not talking about them, I'm talking about you!"

She drew in a deep breath that caught in the middle, and Rex flung the broken stick aside and got to his feet. He was still painfully aroused, and he wasn't going to be able to do a damned thing about it, and it was all her fault for falling in the river!

"I wouldn't mind," she whispered. "I'd like to, in fact. With you."

Now, for the first time in a lot of years, Rex recalled what he'd said to her then. Recalled it, and wished to hell he could go back and live those few minutes all over again. Even back then, when there was little he wouldn't do to flaunt conventions, he had never deliberately hurt anyone.

But given a second chance, he wouldn't have taken his frustration out on a vulnerable kid whose only sin was that she wasn't experienced, either.

"You should be so lucky," he'd sneered. "Babe, for your information, I've got more broads lined up and waiting than I have time to service. Take a number, get in line and wait your turn."

The sound of a blaring horn brought him out of the past, and Rex turned his attention forcefully to the present, counting himself lucky that some shotgun-toting papa hadn't put an end to his career as a wild young stud before it had even got off the ground.

That had been the beginning, though, for him and Carrie. Within the week, she had been his, but to his dying day, he would always remember that day in March when she had begged him and he had so crudely turned her down. Even now he cringed at the memory.

He glanced at her now, at her short, straight nose, at the full lips and stubborn little chin. Had she forgotten? It had been a long time ago, and they'd both done a lot of living in the meantime. But selfishly, he hoped she still remembered every minute they had spent together. God knows, he did.

"Doesn't it look to you like those clouds are clearing away?" she asked, as if aware that she had his attention again. "Maybe Pete and Ody can get the wheat in after all."

"I wouldn't count on it. This time of year, about all you can figure on is being surprised."

"Thanks for the words of encouragement."

The road signs announced a town a quarter of a mile ahead, and Rex signaled a turn. "We're stopping?" she asked.

"You need some dry clothes before you catch cold."

You'd think he had insulted her from the way she reacted. "These will dry! If you're embarrassed to be seen with me in blue jeans, then you shouldn't have bothered to stop in the first place!"

"Give it a rest, will you? We'll melt if I turn off the A/C, but you're freezing in those wet jeans."

"I'm not buying anything, even if you do stop!" She emphasized the words with her left hand, and Rex reached over and captured it, placing it on his thigh and holding it there.

"Carrie, don't be so stiff-necked. You're wet, you're sticky, and if we end up having to spend another night on the road, you're going to need a few things. Naturally, I'll foot the bill for whatever you need, since Billy—"

"You'll do no such thing! All right, if you're so set on making me change my clothes, there's a discount store. I can get anything I need there."

"Make you a deal. You go to the drugstore and get yourself a toothbrush and whatever, and I'll pick out something comfortable for you to travel in."

"Do you make a habit of buying clothes for all your women?'

"Do you make a habit of arguing with all your men over every little thing they try to do for you?'

Stalemate. Rex circled the half-empty parking lot, pulled into a slot close to the small row of stores and switched off the engine. When the air conditioner went off, they were immediately smote by early-afternoon heat. "Do we have a bargain?" he ventured.

Carrie knew she was being childish—she even knew why. There weren't enough weapons in her entire arsenal to arm her against falling under this man's spell again. She couldn't afford to take the risk. "You never answered my question," she parried.

"Which one? About buying women's clothes?"

"You know what I mean," she mumbled, unable to look at him.

"Are you still trying to find out if I'm married?" He had to laugh at her quick denial. "I'm not now, nor have I ever been married, okay? That doesn't mean there haven't been women in my life, and yes, I've been known to buy clothes for a few of them. What's the matter, don't you trust my taste?"

"Don't be absurd," she muttered, trying hard not to let her relief show. *He wasn't married! He might be involved, but at least he wasn't married!* "I'll buy my own clothes," she pronounced, and Rex let it go at that. He had an idea she was skirting pretty close to the edge, financially. He'd like to spare her the expense if he could figure a way around that damnable pride of hers.

Some twenty minutes later, Rex caught sight of a familiar redhead striding across the parking lot, swinging a lumpy plastic carrier. She was wearing a full skirt in a gaudy print of hot pink, orange and yellow, with an orange blouse. It should have looked abominable with her flaming hair, but somehow, it didn't. On her feet were a pair of hot-pink platform sandals that hoisted her up a good two inches from the pavement, and when she came close enough, he could see that she was sporting a pair of dangling pink plastic earrings roughly the size and shape of a couple of Vienna sausages.

"If you're trying to get my attention, lady, you have it." Holding open the passenger door, he bowed her in, grinning. "I won't even ask what color nightgown you bought."

"You needn't. I wouldn't tell you even if I'd bought one."

"Am I going to get to see it?" he teased, recognizing her defiant mood as sheer defensiveness.

"In your dreams," she cracked, and he chuckled.

"Sweetheart, you don't know how right you are. We can stop off at a launderette and wash your jeans and shirt if you want to."

"Have you forgotten why we're here? This might be a vacation for you, but I've got to find Kim and get her back home before Daddy blows a gasket."

"Just thought I'd offer."

"Yes, well . . . thank you."

He began to chuckle. "That hurt, didn't it?"

"I don't know what you're talking about."

"Thanking me."

"You're being perfectly absurd. I've always thanked you whenever you did me a favor, and you know it."

The laughter ended. "I can remember one time when you didn't. That day when you fell in the river, when I—"

She caught her breath audibly. "Don't," she whispered. "Let's just remember why we're here and forget—"

"Forget what, Carrie? Forget that once we were lovers?"

"I've already forgotten that."

"Yeah. Sure you have. Just like I have." Rex flexed his shoulders and adjusted the angle of his seat. Why did he go on jabbing at her? It wasn't fair to either of them. The trouble was, he knew her too well. Knew exactly which buttons to push to set her off, and found himself pushing them whenever she started to get to him. Whenever he started raking up too many memories.

And especially whenever she tried to deny what was between them.

Okay, so it might not be a rational response. As long as it worked, he was going to use it, because where Carrie was concerned, he'd learned a long time ago that it was far too easy to get in over his head.

Five
————

Three hours should have done it, probably would have if Rex hadn't suddenly decided to leave the Interstate. Two wrecks and an increasing number of vehicles headed south was the determining factor, and when Carrie questioned him about it, he claimed it was also more direct.

"More congested, too," she countered, and they were off again. A small part of her brain remarked on the fact that there seemed to be no middle ground for them. Either they were at each other's throats or...

Or in each other's arms, she thought irrelevantly. And they weren't. Not really. If it felt that way, it was only wishful thinking on her part. For so long she'd dreamed about meeting him again, and looking so beautiful that he wouldn't be able to resist her this time.

So now she'd met him again, wearing her dirty, everyday work clothes, and when she'd had a chance to replace them with something soft and feminine, she'd got her back up and bought the gaudiest outfit in the store. It was called cutting off one's nose to spite one's face, and Carrie was very good at it. If he still found her every bit as resistible as he had fifteen years ago—and obviously, he did—she had only herself to blame.

"You know, it's a wonder we haven't bumped into each other before now, what with your dad's place being right across the river from my cabin," Rex observed. He glanced at her profile and his eyes lingered on her full bottom lip.

"Not really. We don't run cattle on that strip on account of all the wild cherry trees along the river. They're poison to cattle, you know. Besides, it's so rocky there, a fall would be risky."

Rex fell silent. He should have gone back for her sooner. How could he have let her go so easily? But then, when a guy was seventeen, with one man threatening to geld him and another one threatening him with reform school if he got a girl in trouble, he tended to pull in his horns if he was at all smart.

Carrie had still been a child in the eyes of her family. And in the eyes of the law, he reminded himself bitterly. Trust his old man to bring up that particular delicate point.

"If you're bound to screw up," John Ryder had roared, "at least do it with some chippy who won't land you in court on a statutory rape charge! God, sometimes I wonder why the hell I ever bothered to take you on in the first place! If Elizabeth hadn't talked me into it . . ."

Which hadn't helped his state of mind at the time, Rex remembered bleakly.

But the past was already written in indelible ink, he reminded himself impatiently. He'd do better to let it go.

Placing another call to his friend in Durham, he outlined the current status, snapped out a couple of directives and promised to check back in a couple of hours.

"Who's Steve?" Carrie asked.

"Hacker friend of mine."

"A hacker? You mean he coughs a lot?'

"No, I mean he uses an electronic passkey to find out what he wants to know." Briefly he explained what a hacker did.

"Is that legal?"

"Legality's optional. As far as I know, Steve keeps it pretty much on the level."

"And if he doesn't, you don't want to know about it, right?'

Rex shrugged.

Carrie sniffed. "So much for your high-sounding position with the department of justice," she said dryly.

"Steve's quicker, and a hell of a lot more private. I don't wash my personal laundry at public expense."

"Or in public washrooms," Carrie added.

"You got it." He watched his chance and passed a farm tractor while Carrie eyed the condition of the fields. By the time they dried up enough for a tractor to get in there, it would probably be too late.

"Kim wants to go to New York and try to become a model." Rex arched a dark eyebrow, but didn't comment. He hadn't counted on all the farm traffic. Not to mention the Sunday-afternoon motorists out for a leisurely airing. "Daddy won't let her, of course. Not that she's not pretty enough, but New York! Lord, he'd have a fit!"

"It's urban. It's northern. It's not necessarily fatal." Privately, he thought Ralph Lanier would dig in his heels if either of his daughters tried to escape. He'd probably only allowed Carrie to marry his manager because he thought it would tie them both to the farm.

Carrie talked some more about her sister, about wanting her to go into nurses' training, hoping after this fling she'd be ready to settle down to something practical.

Once more, Rex spared her his opinion. Personally, he doubted very much that an eighteen-year-old girl with visions of being a New York model would be ready to settle for something as practical as nursing. In any case, he was more interested in Carrie's future than her sister's. She was no longer married, but she was a long way from being free. He tested and discarded several questions, then asked, "What will you do when your father retires? Take over the farm from him?"

"I don't think farmers ever really retire. A few sell out, but mostly they either go broke or hand over the reins to a son."

"Or daughter," he said dryly.

She didn't bother to reply to that, but it wasn't necessary. Ralph Lanier wasn't the kind of man who would hand over his lifetime's work to a woman, even if she was his own daughter—a daughter who had evidently worked her butt off so he wouldn't lose his precious farm.

He flexed his shoulders. The needle on the speedometer edged farther to the right. To think he was considered a topnotch fraud investigator in certain circles, used to picking up a single clue, following a tortuous electronic trail to the bitter end and coming out the winner. He had a reputation for making collars that stuck like Super Glue, but he was beginning to find out that matching wits via computer was a hell of a lot different from this one-on-one business. Especially when one of the ones was a woman who could turn him on by simply breathing!

"When do you call your hacker friend back?" she asked after a dozen miles had gone by in silence.

For an answer, Rex reached for the phone again. Like all cellulars, it was simplex rather than duplex, so she was privy to only one end of the conversation, and that ran to mono-syllables.

"Well?" she asked when he'd signed off.

"Nothing."

"What do you mean, nothing?"

"Nothing we can use, at least."

Her hands took off like a pair of startled doves. "Didn't he tell you *anything?*"

"Yeah. They're not back home, they're not dead, they're not in the pokey, and they're not in a hospital, okay? If you happen to know your sister's driver's license number, maybe I can dig a little deeper. A social security number would work, but it's not as direct."

"What do you mean, direct?'

And then he had to explain about personal identification numbers, and PIN terminals, and how the system worked, which took up another few miles.

"Well, I'm sorry, but I don't know any of Kim's num-bers. I don't even know my own."

"That figures," he snapped, angry with himself, taking it out on her.

Impatiently, Carrie said, "Look, they can't just have disappeared off the face of the earth! Aren't you the least bit worried? What if they're really in trouble? What if they picked up a hitchhiker and he did something awful and—"

Sighing, Rex reached an arm across her shoulder, mut-tered an oath directed at the designer of bucket seats and then said, "Okay, I'm worried. Does that make you feel better? Believe it or not, most kids run away from home because they're bored, or scared, or just plain miserable. Maybe they just want to find themselves. Instead, they end up getting even more lost. At least with Kim and Billy, we can be pretty sure of their motives, which means we can be pretty sure they're safe, wherever they are.''

"Safe," she repeated bitterly. "You mean chances are, Billy won't be the one to wind up getting pregnant and having to—"

"Dammit, there are a lot of things worse than pregnancy!"

"I just said so, didn't I?" she stormed right back.

"Look on the bright side." The curl of his mobile lips suggested that the side he was looking on was anything but bright. "Thirty-four years ago another couple of kids slipped up, and because of their mistake, I'm here now. So don't ask me to figure out the grand scheme of things, lady. Believe me, I've tried!"

Carrie turned a pair of stricken brown eyes on him, and Rex swore. He didn't usually spout off this way. She had this effect on him—always had. He found himself wanting to forget the rest of the world, wanting to hold her, to burrow his hands through her hair, to kiss away her fears, her worries, and make everything come out right for her.

Hell, he couldn't even make things come out right for himself. If it had been that easy, he'd have long since headed for the nearest bed to begin making up for all the lost years, Kim and Billy bedamned!

Regretting his irritability—regretting a lot of things—Rex dropped his arm and placed his hand on her thigh, squeezing gently. "Sorry if I sounded like a bear with his tail caught in a crack, honey. I'm not always this—" He braked as a funeral procession pulled out in front of them, and then drove at a dogged thirty-five miles an hour for the next five minutes.

Carrie nibbled a thumbnail. She twitched. "I told you the Interstate would've been quicker. At least you could've passed."

"All right, you told me so," Rex said evenly.

But Carrie had bottled up too much for too long. "Well, it's the truth! If you had a grain of common sense, we'd have been there by now, and—"

"If I had a grain of common sense I'd never have stopped to pick you up in the first place! In which case you'd still be at a garage in Charlotte waiting for that piece of junk you call a truck to be patched up!"

"Oh, yeah! Well, if you hadn't practically kidnapped me right off the highway, I'd have rented a car and found them by now!"

"Sure, at the Mimosa Palace, right?'

"It's *Terrace!* Mimosa Terrace, and it's not my fault they weren't there!" She glowered at him, and Rex immediately relented. It occurred to him that tempers weren't the only things that were suffering. His body was suffering from a bad case of old-fashioned frustrated lust, and as for Carrie, he had a pretty good idea that her wallet was running on empty. She had a tow charge to pay and a truck to get out of hock, and from what she'd let drop in their more peaceable moments, running a small cattle operation was a shaky business at the best of times. He knew of more than one high roller who used his farm as a tax write-off, at least they had until the tax forms had been simplified beyond all comprehension. Unless he missed his guess, Ralph Lanier had never rolled much above the break-even point. Which might help account for some of his daughter's porcupine pride.

"Look, Carrie, I—"

"Forget it! I don't want to be here any more than you want me here, so the sooner we get done with this business, the sooner we can each go our own way!"

Which was just what he was afraid of. Guiltily, Rex knew he was going to string things out as long as he could. If Billy was determined to get in over his head, he'd had plenty of time to do it. Meanwhile, Rex had Carrie back again, and this time there was nobody around to louse things up for him.

Not that he needed any help on that score.

Sensing a change in his mood, Carrie watched him from the corner of her eye. Behind those dark glasses, it was impossible to tell if he was aware of being studied. She was almost past caring. This might just be the last chance she would ever have to look her fill at that rugged, beautiful face. "Sorry I blew up," she said quietly.

"Me, too. I guess we're both pretty strung out."

She let it go at that. Traffic was light, but of the sporadic type that had to be watched constantly. A car pulled out of a driveway right in front of them, causing Rex to slam on the brakes, and then turned off again before he was even done swearing. Carrie didn't make the mistake of saying I-told-you-so. Not a second time.

She'd almost forgotten just how shockingly attractive he was! Neither the squint lines around his eyes and the deepened grooves bracketing his mouth, nor the trace of gray in his tar-brown hair, made any difference. He looked every bit as beautiful and dangerous as he had fifteen years ago. Even more. Maturity lent him a certain sureness that he had lacked then—not that she'd been aware he'd lacked it at the time.

At fifteen she'd been no match for him. Would she fare any better as a thirty-year-old divorcée? She couldn't afford to find out. Take a number and wait, he'd told her once upon a time. That had been the beginning of it all. Idly, Carrie wondered what number he was on now.

Twenty minutes later, Rex tried placing another call to Hilton Head, only to find that half the lines in southeast South Carolina were dead. He tried another number and learned that entire banks of computers were also down, thanks to a couple of predawn storms that had ripped through three states.

"Next time those two pull a stunt like this, I hope to hell they pick a safer month," he grumbled.

"For instance?"

"February!"

"Ice storms," she reminded him.

"October, then."

"Hurricane season's not over."

He grimaced. "You're a regular bundle of sunshine, aren't you?"

Carrie bit back a smile and told herself that they could still be friends, in spite of the past. But it wasn't true. They might make a show of pretending otherwise, but they both knew that it would never work. There was a barrier between them now that hadn't been there when they were younger, and no matter how much she might want to pretend it didn't exist, Carrie was too much of a realist. Joanna and Don had never got along, but it wouldn't help matters at this stage in her life to bring home a stranger and announce that he was Joanna's real father.

As they sped south toward the Ryders' summer place, Carrie shifted restlessly in her soft leather seat. She unfolded the crumpled road map she'd dug out of the glove compartment and then refolded it along the proper creases. They passed a herd that looked like it might be a Charolais-Hereford cross, and she sized up their general age, sex and condition. She counted blue trucks and Georgia license plates, and when that palled, she began mentally estimating the weights of her own fall calves.

Anxiously, she glanced at her leather-strapped watch, as if time had any real meaning. Yesterday she'd planned on beginning the two-hundred-five-day weighing and measuring, hoping to finish before the combining started. She only hoped Ody could hold the fort. He was old and ornery—sometimes she thought he'd been born that way—and Pete would probably choose this weekend to go off on a toot. There was never any end to it. Never any answers.

Desperately, she tried to ignore the man beside her, to pretend that he was someone she'd just met, someone who didn't matter other than he was Billy's brother, and wherever Billy was, Kim was, too.

It was hopeless. She could smell the scent of his aftershave, hear the sound of his breathing and feel the warmth radiating from his big hard body. Had he forgotten she was here? she wondered. If he had a single thought beyond controlling all this fancy horsepower, he hid it well. Of all the men in the world for her sister to get involved with, why did it have to be Rex's little brother?

By the time they stopped for lunch, the sky to the west had turned a putrid shade of olive drab. Thunder rumbled ominously in the distance, and a few dusty trees flipped their leaves to reveal their silver-gray undersides.

"Drive-in suit you? We're almost there, and I'd just as soon get on down the road."

Carrie nodded. She was starving, but she didn't think she could eat a bite. She uttered a sound that was somewhere between a laugh and a sigh, and unexpectedly, Rex closed his strong fingers over her arm in a gesture of reassurance. "Worried about the kids or the weather?" he asked gently.

"Both, I guess."

"If it's any comfort to you, I doubt if they'll be spending much time on the beach."

"Oh, thanks a lot!" she said with a broken little laugh.

Rex pulled into the drive-up line, captured her left hand and began tracing the row of calluses at the base of her fingers with his thumb. "You worry too much, short stuff.

There's a billiard table at the cottage—a pretty good library, too, if I remember correctly. Must've come with the house, because I've never seen Stella crack anything heavier than *Town and Country* magazine.''

Carrie smiled halfheartedly, but neither of them seriously thought the younger couple would spare much time for books or billiards. It was all too obvious to Rex what Carrie was thinking. Hell, he was thinking the same thing. Was she remembering all those times by the river? The time she had got a tick on her waist and he'd had to back it out with a match head and then kiss the spot to make it well? One thing had led to another. And then another...

Rex leaned back, looking suddenly tired, and it occurred to Carrie that he must be just as worried as she was. Billy's mother probably had some snippy little debutante all picked out for her precious son. She was probably having conniption fits by now.

Almost as if he'd read her mind, Rex said, "Carrie, has it ever occurred to you that there might be some significance to this birthday business? You said Kim had just turned eighteen."

"Significance? You mean because she wanted me to give her a week at the beach with a friend? I told you, that's why I was so sure they were at Myrtle. It's where all her friends go the week school lets out."

He dismissed that notion with an impatient gesture, placed an order for drinks, bacon-cheeseburgers and fries without consulting her, and said, "Look, doesn't it strike you as significant that they took off for South Carolina the very day Kim turned eighteen? Think about it. What's this state known for?"

"Fireworks? The shag? Beach music? Boiled peanuts? No, that's Georgia, isn't it?"

The girl at the window handed over a large sack, and Carrie reached for her purse.

Rex shook his head. He paid the tab and then pulled away from the window. "Marriage mills. Get a license, wait twenty-four hours and bingo."

Carrie took a moment to digest the notion. She felt in the sack and came up with a french fry. Nibbling absently, she considered a wealth of new possibilities, none of them promising. "Bingo?"

Rex waited for her synapses to put through the message. He watched as she felt in the bag for another french fry, and then dropped it untasted. "Oh, God, not bingo," she whispered.

"Yeah. Kind of puts another face on things, doesn't it?"

"Especially if they're pregnant," she murmured. Unwrapping her bacon-cheeseburger, she laid it on the dashboard, untouched.

"Especially if they're pregnant," Rex concurred. "Kids having kids, leaving them to twist in the wind while the marriage goes sour. Billy ought to know better."

"Maybe you're wrong. Maybe they just wanted to get away somewhere together," Carrie suggested. A notion that had been totally unacceptable only a few hours ago suddenly seemed so benign.

Rex pulled back onto the highway, and without asking, Carrie unwrapped his burger, folded the paper down and handed it to him. "I think we're going to have to accept that marriage is a possibility, if not a probability," he said, nodding his thanks without taking his eye off the road. "That's what I was trying to check out when I found out the lines were down."

"But...marriage! Kim's nowhere near ready for that kind of responsibility."

The corners of Rex's mouth turned down in a bitter smile. "You think Billy is? He still lives on an allowance from his mother. He thinks the height of responsibility is rolling up the windows of his Mustang when it looks like it might rain."

"Kim still sleeps with a rag doll. She can't even cook."

"Can she thaw?"

"That's the trouble, I'm afraid she already has." Carrie smiled and Rex chuckled, but there was more resignation than amusement in both reactions.

They were both silent for a while, deep in their own thoughts as Rex headed for the turnoff to Hilton Road. "I should've spent more time with her," Carrie said. "But Jo takes up any free time I have. Lib's always busy, and Daddy doesn't have a lick of patience. Still, I should've found the time somehow. She needed me, and I—"

"Don't blame yourself, honey."

The tenderness in Rex's voice might have undone her if she'd heard it, but Carrie was too busy burying herself under layers of guilt. "It's just that she's always still asleep when I leave the house in the morning, and then either she's got a date or Jo needs help with her homework. Or I've got a Cattleman's Association meeting, or I'm snowed under with office work."

"Office work?"

Carrie's gaze fastened unseeingly on the sacks of feed in the back of the pickup in front of them. "You wouldn't believe the paperwork involved in running a beef operation." She reached into the sack for a french fry, came up empty and frowned, as if she couldn't quite remember what it was she'd been reaching for. "Still, I could have tried harder. I should have reminded her about—about Mama and Daddy, and how they'd had to get married, and how it had ruined everything for them both. I should have encouraged her to confide in me, but whenever she wanted to talk, there was always something else I had to do."

"If I thought marriage would make Billy grow up, I wouldn't mind so much," Rex said after a silence that felt surprisingly companionable. "Kids that age have so damn many strikes against them. If they're pregnant, that's doubled in spades."

"She'll feel trapped."

"He'll feel tied down."

After a few minutes, Rex said, "Of course, if Billy were a few years older, it might not be all that bad. Marriage, I mean. With the right woman."

"Kim's never going to make it as a model. She's only five feet four. And I don't really think she'll go for nursing. Actually, at this point, she's not interested in much of anything but clothes and Billy."

"What were you like at eighteen, Carrie? I often wondered."

At eighteen she'd been busy keeping the farm books, taking care of a recklessly independent toddler, placating an abusive husband and trying to mend a broken heart in her spare time. "Busy," she said.

Busy. Rex smiled, his eyes wintery. At eighteen he had still been hung up on proving himself and getting back to Carrie. Even after he'd discovered that there was nothing to go back to, he would find himself thinking of her at the damnedest times. Back in high school, once he'd met Carrie, he had begun to grow bored with the kind of girls who had once attracted him. Later in life, he'd been drawn to a certain kind of woman—women with guts, a complete lack of malice and a quirky sense of humor.

The fact that most of them just happened to be redheaded was probably coincidental. "Is that it?" He prompted. "Just . . . busy? Busy doing what?"

"You asked for it," she said, grinning. "I just hope it doesn't put you to sleep." Her eyes lingered for a while on his sharply chiseled profile. She'd always considered it the height of perfection, broken nose and all.

"I'll risk it."

She screwed up her face, and Rex, catching a glimpse of her, had to smile. When Carrie concentrated, she threw her whole body into it. But then, she'd never done anything by half measures. He happened to know she'd been driving a tractor ever since she was knee-high to a cricket—not that she was much bigger than that now. He could easily picture her wrestling several tons of farm equipment around Lanier's rugged fields.

"I didn't go to college, you know," she confessed self-consciously. "Mostly I was too busy with the apartment and the baby and the farm and everything to think about it, but sometimes I wished—I mean, I wondered . . ."

"I'm sorry, Carrie."

"It happens. I doubt if I missed all that much. We had a nice apartment, and there was Jo. Being a wife and a mother and a part-time farm worker doesn't leave a whole lot of time to ponder things like making your first million or saving the planet."

"What happened to your marriage?'

"It sort of—dwindled out, I guess."

"Why?" Like a sore tooth, he had to keep probing to know where the pain was and how bad it could get.

"Don discovered that he didn't care for marriage." He also discovered that, after all, he didn't really want a child who wasn't his or a woman who was still in love with someone else. "It wasn't really his fault."

Carrie tucked one foot beneath her and tried to think of a way to divert his attention before he stumbled onto the truth. "I could never have borrowed his toothbrush, you know. I should've known from that that it wouldn't last."

"Borrowed his *what?*"

"Toothbrush. It's a test. All the girls in high school said it was the best test for true love, and Don and I flunked it."

Rex favored her with a bemused look. "Flunked the acid test, huh?"

"No, the toothbrush test," she said gravely. Rex began to chuckle and after a moment, so did she.

But soon she was frowning again, and Rex figured she was worrying over her sister. He offered what he hoped would be a comforting thought. "Lots of kids marry young, Carrie. Sometimes it works out."

"Mostly it doesn't."

"We both have reason to wish they'd waited until they were older, but maybe it's still not too late." Rex thought about his own reasons, and then he thought about hers. A bad marriage, a couple of kids deserted by their mother. On top of that there had been her father's accident. Rex had a pretty good idea who had borne the brunt of it all. Carrie probably didn't weigh a hundred pounds soaking wet, bust, butt and steel backbone included, but he'd lay odds she was more than a match for Ralph Lanier.

"Your Dad must've had his accident pretty soon after I left town."

"The same year, in fact. He'd decided to clear off that riverside piece so we could run a herd on it, and he rolled the tractor."

"How's he managing now?"

"Oh, fine. Lib spoils him rotten at home, and he has a golf cart with balloon tires for getting around the farm. Rex, weren't we supposed to turn off back there? The sign said Bluffton, and according to the map—"

He swore, she flinched, and then he wanted to apologize. But dammit, she had him so screwed up, first with this Don guy, and then wondering how he was going to get her away from her old man. And how long he was going to be able to keep himself from pulling over to the side of the road and kissing her silly, right there on the right-of-way! "If you'd quit distracting me, maybe I could keep my mind on what I'm doing," he muttered, aware that he was being grossly unfair, embarrassed because he'd been half-aroused ever since he'd seen her in his T-shirt that morning. "I'm sorry, Carrie. I don't know what gets into me. I'm generally a pretty sweet guy."

Her jaw was set, her color high, and Rex pulled off onto the shoulder and leaned his head back for a moment. "I really am sorry, honey. I didn't get much sleep last night, and—"

"Oh, and that's my fault, too, I suppose!"

"I didn't say that. If you want to put the blame somewhere, blame it on the weather. It's hot as blazes, and unless I miss my guess, we're going to catch hell before we get back home."

"That's supposing we find Kim and Billy at Hilton Head."

Still feeling edgy, Rex gave her a long look. She was staring straight ahead with that stubborn little chin of hers thrust forward the way he'd seen her jut it out a hundred times in the past. For all her volatility, her defenses were pathetically inadequate. Always had been. On the other hand, he'd seen her tackle a hulking quarterback twice her size when he'd mouthed off about pneumatic breasts. She'd demolished him with a few well-chosen, cattle-related phrases.

"Carrie, I'm sorry. That's all I can say."

Her fists were clenched in her lap, and he reached out and covered them with one hand. She stiffened. When her lower lip quivered, he felt a dam begin to crumble inside him, a dam that had been carefully and painfully constructed over a period of years. "Honey, would you just look at me? Please?"

She did, her face wiped clean of all expression.

Rex realized he was sweating. The air conditioner was running, but it was fighting a losing battle against the elements. Switching off the engine, he rolled down a window, and his senses were immediately inundated by the heavy sweetness of a grove of blooming privet smothered under honeysuckle vines.

Carrie sniffed. She swore and sniffed again, and then she sneezed six times in a row. "Oh, dabbit, dot dow!"

Dabbit dot dow? "Come again?" Rex murmured.

She glared at him and sneezed again.

"Oh, hell, you're allergic! I clean forgot!" He rolled up the window and switched on the air conditioner just as the rumble of thunder sounded.

"I'b owdly allergic to certaid blossobs. I have sub bedicide, but I forgot to take it this bordi'g."

"Let's get moving. You need something to take a pill with, right?"

"If you dod't bide too buch."

Rex began to grin. Then he began to chuckle. "Hey, an allergy like that is nothing to sneeze at, right?"

She socked him on the shoulder with a surprisingly hard little fist, but then she began to laugh, too. "That's a horrid joke!"

"Yeah, I know. Your favorite kind, right?"

They were both silent while Rex got them back on the proper route, but each was remembering a time when they'd saved jokes to share with each other—the more atrocious, the better. "We'll be there before long, Carrie. How do you want to handle it?"

"How cad I dough that whed I dodn't dough what we'll fide."

"First, we'll find something for you to take your medicine with," he said as he pulled into a service station.

A few minutes later he was back with an icy drink. Carrie swallowed the prescription antihistamine she carried in her purse and thanked him. "Rex, I'b sorry I acted so silly. You were right. If I hadn't distracted you, you'd never have bissed that—"

"Hey, wait a minute, don't hog all the guilt for yourself, lady. I was the one who asked you to distract me, remember?"

"I could've givved you the short versiod."

Against a background of thunder, soft music and the purr of a well-behaved engine, he said, "So give it to me now."

"Too late, you've already had the log wod. Oh, I hate talking whed by does is stopped up!"

"Your ears aren't stopped up, are they? I noticed you didn't ask what I've doing all this time? Aren't you even interested?"

He quirked a sooty eyebrow, and Carrie felt an old familiar weakness invade her bones. She blew her nose, took a few experimental breaths and said, "I already know. Going to school. Racking up degrees. Rushing all over the state fighting evildoers with your trusty computers."

"You snooped."

"Billy brags."

"Oh. I was hoping you'd been curious." His smile ate a hole in her defenses a mile wide. "Short stuff," he said, unconsciously using the pet name he'd tacked on her back in high school. "Do you think you're ready for whatever we find? They might not even be there, you know. But if they're married, ten to one, Billy'll take her there for the honeymoon.''

"What if we find them in time? What do we do then?"

"Try to talk some sense into their heads. You feel up to it?"

"Even with my head cleared up, I'm better with cows than people."

Rex smiled, and the warmth of it made her toes curl. "That's a lot of bull, and you know it."

"You know, I didn't realize how much I've missed you all these years." *Oh, no. I didn't really say that out loud, did I?*

Lightning flashed, and Carrie wondered if electricity in the atmosphere could short-circuit a person's brain. "Your jokes, I mean. I miss your jokes."

"I know what you mean, Carrie," he said quietly. "Me, too, for what it's worth."

Six

Rex drove past the golf course, past the tennis court, and pulled into the circular driveway of a magnificent pink house centered among pine trees, azaleas and camellias. Out of the corner of his eye he saw Carrie clasp her hands tightly in her lap. Her feet in the ridiculous hot-pink sandals were flat on the carpeted floor, pressed tightly together, and she was sitting as erect as her shoulder harness allowed.

"Atten—*tion!* Eyes right," he commanded softly, and she gasped audibly. "Sorry, I couldn't resist. Hey, relax, okay? We're going to take it one step at a time and deal with it as we go."

"I am relaxed!" It was patently untrue, but he didn't argue.

He glanced around. "Hmm. Place doesn't look too lively from here. Want to go with me to check things out or wait in the car?"

"I'll wait here. In case..." She let it drop, and Rex swung himself out of the car, leaned back inside and gave her a reassuring thumbs-up sign.

He took his time, circled the place twice, checking everything. Five minutes later, he slid into the car again. "Locked up tight as a tick. Storm blinds, pool cover, doors, garage—everything. No sign of life."

"Don't say that, not even as a joke!"

"Honey, they're not here, that's all. We'll find them."

"I know that." Her eyes were too bright, her smile unconvincing. "But they weren't where I thought they'd be, and now they're not where you thought they'd be. What else is left? Do we stick a pin in the map? Or roll dice? Or maybe go find us a fortune-teller?"

"We think. I see if the phones are back on line, and then we go get the biggest ice-cream cones we can find and race to see if we can finish them off before they melt and drip all over us."

"You're really and truly not worried, then?" she asked anxiously, and Rex shook his head.

Hell yes, he was worried, but worrying wasn't going to help, and falling apart had never been his style. Besides, she was counting on him. The way he saw it, what she needed now more than anything else was to be distracted until he could figure out their next move. If she had any idea of the possibilities that had gone through his mind from the time he first heard they were missing, they'd both probably be crying in their beer.

Billy was the closest thing to family Rex had. Not Belinda. There had never been any real closeness between them, even when he'd believed her to be his real sister. Certainly not Stella, who had insisted on shipping him off to boarding school, strictly for his own good, as she'd said.

But Billy had come along later, and blood kin or not, the bond had formed early. God knows what the kid had seen in him, but he'd seen in Billy someone to care about, to look after. Someone whose eyes had lighted up, who had chortled in his Pablum whenever Rex walked into the room.

Stella had hated it. Billy was her baby, and she didn't like competing for his affections. Reacting predictably, she had shipped Rex off to school again, but he'd kept on bouncing back. It was only when Billy got old enough to begin playing off one adult against the other that Rex had quit trying to interfere, but even now he kept in touch. He still cared, and he wanted to believe that Billy did, too.

"Did you say something about ice cream?" Carrie reminded him once they'd left the palatial pink beach house behind. Lost in thought, Rex had automatically headed for the bridge.

"Sure did. If memory serves, we'll find a freezerful right down this street."

Memory served. "Still chocolate?" he asked.

"Still chocolate."

A few minutes later they were parked in the shade, licking the melting edges of their triple cones. "So how do you like Stella's cozy little cottage?" Rex asked.

Carrie darted her tongue out to catch a milky dribble, and Rex stared at her glistening mouth, momentarily transfixed. "If that's a cottage, my name is Calvin Coolidge."

Rex switched on the engine and set the air conditioner for Arctic blast. "Well, Cal, you know what they say. Different strokes for different folks." He grinned, his gray eyes watching as she struggled to maintain some kind of damage control on her rapidly melting cone.

"Make mine sidestrokes in a calm sea. I guess your family prefers to take their strokes on a golf course."

"It's honest work. Somebody has to stuff balls in all those little holes in the ground." Opening the door, he leaned out and disposed of the remnants of his cone, and then removed hers from her grasp while he dug out a handkerchief. "Hold still, hmm? You've got this little place... right... here." Taking her chin between the thumb and forefinger of the hand that held the handkerchief, he looked helplessly at the other one that held her dripping cone and then shrugged. "Mother of invention, I guess," he murmured, and before she knew what he meant to do, he was doing it.

It wasn't exactly a kiss, but it wasn't exactly *not* a kiss, either. Carrie's breath caught and held as she felt the hot velvet tip of his tongue at the corner of her mouth. He stroked his way slowly across to the other corner, pausing to nibble along the way, and then, for one long moment, he pressed his mouth against her, not seeking entrance, not even moving. His eyes were open, and so were hers. Carrie, staring at the fuzzy, out-of-focus image of warm tanned skin, gleaming black hair and cool gray eyes, absorbed the very essence of Rex Ryder into her soul in that single time-out-of-time.

Slowly, Rex lifted his face away, stared intently into her eyes as she gradually came to grips with the world around her. Then, matter-of-factly, he tucked the handkerchief into his pocket and handed back her cone. "There, I think that's got it," he said. "No, golf was never my game, either. I still enjoy bodysurfing, though. Did you ever get around to trying it?'

Carrie scrambled madly for the appearance, at least, of composure. He couldn't know that her heart was beating its wings madly against her rib cage, that her lungs had collapsed, and that any minute now, the fire in her lower body was going to set off a smoke alarm. "Ah—well, personally,

I prefer lazing on the balcony at the Mimosa Terrace. It's not right on the ocean, but at least you can wake up in the middle of the night when the traffic dies down and hear the surf swishing on the shore. And of course, there's the smell . . ."

"That tangy, iodine-y smell, you mean." *God, man, you had to go and taste her mouth again! Keep it up and you'll be shopping for an pair of stainless steel briefs!*

She must have said something that made sense, but all he could hear was the husky sound of her voice and the sound of his own blood rampaging through his circulatory system. Struggling to put his brain back on line, he said, "Y-know, when you get right down to it, the most important thing in a beach house is windows that open. A few well-placed ceiling fans are always welcome. Maybe some sand on the floor for atmosphere. And of course, a place to tie up a boat."

"I've never had a boat so I wouldn't know about that, but the gritty floors I can do without."

"Gritty floors are a necessary part of the beach mystique." He shifted in his seat, angled the air vent to a lower position and did a slow breathing exercise designed to calm hyperactive nerves

"As you said," Carrie murmured. "Different strokes."

They fell silent, both lost in their own thoughts. Carrie repeated silently, "I *am* the master of my fate," and a few other highflown sentiments. For all the good it did her.

Sex! You'd think it was the most important thing in the world!

A bit grimly, she said, "If you don't mind, I'd like to check in with Lib again. I promised to keep her posted, not that there's much to report."

Rex placed the call, got through with no hitch and handed over the receiver. He listened unabashedly while Carrie learned that the combining crew was planning to start first thing in the morning, and that Ralph had pitched a fit because she wasn't there to oversee the operation, and that the timer on the washing machine had gone crazy and would have to be replaced and since it was twenty-two years old, the parts were no longer available.

She handed back the receiver and said, "Lib didn't even ask about Kim, can you believe it?"

"Maybe she thinks whatever an eighteen-year-old girl does with a twenty-one-year-old boy is none of our business."

"She was worried enough before. She said Daddy would blow a gasket if I didn't find Kim and get her back home."

Rex had a pretty good idea which one of them Ralph Lanier was missing most, and it wouldn't be the prima donna who slept late and wanted to go to New York to become a model.

"I hate it that you've had to chase all over the state, but you do understand why, don't you, Rex?" Carrie pleaded.

"Sure, I understand." And he did, too. A single glance at any newspaper would be enough to scare the hell out of the family of a missing teenager.

On the other hand, there'd been no evidence of foul play, no evidence to suggest that this was anything other than what it seemed. A couple of hotheaded kids wanted to shack up together and figured if their parents were worried enough, they'd be glad just to get them back in one piece, and they could get away with it. They were probably right, too.

Carrie lifted her hair away from her neck, and Rex tried not to let himself be distracted by the sight of her soft, pale nape. Where the sun didn't touch her, she had skin the color of whipped cream. Not to mention the texture and the taste.

Swearing under his breath, he reached for his sunglasses and jammed them on his face. The sky, at the moment, was roughly the shade of wet slate.

"Weren't you wanting to place a call, too?"

"Yeah, thanks for reminding me," he muttered. Half a dozen academic degrees, and suddenly he had the attention span of a flea! Great going, Ryder.

The call didn't take long. Carrie, distracted by her own concerns, listened in halfheartedly, trying to glean information from his few terse questions. It sounded like all the other calls he'd placed. Evidently, computer people spoke a language of their own.

He turned to her and said, "That's Kimberly Ann Lanier, right?"

Carrie nodded. Naturally anyone looking for them would have to know their names.

"Yeah. Right," Rex said to the unknown party on the other end. And then he removed his glasses and slung them onto the dash, his brows lowered over slits of silvery gray. "When?" he barked.

For a moment after he replaced the receiver, he didn't say anything. Carrie's imagination leaped into overdrive, and her face lost color. By the time he turned to her, she wasn't even breathing.

"Carrie—" he began.

"They're not—"

"Oh, God, no! Nothing like that!"

Suddenly, she knew what was coming, knew it in her bones. "They're married, aren't they?"

Rex's expression was bleak as he nodded. "Close enough. They took out a license this morning. If they'd done it as soon as they'd hit the state line, we'd have found them by now, but they waited, and then the phone lines went out..."

"And now it's already too late." Suddenly she grabbed his arm, causing him to swerve dangerously. "Rex—this morning, you said? But we can still catch them in time! You said the waiting period was twenty-four hours. That means we've got until tomorrow morning! All we have to do is find out where they've gone to wait it out and talk some sense into them before it's too late!"

"That is if we don't end up wrapped around a telephone pole first."

She winced and removed her hands from his iron-bound forearm. "Oh. Sorry. I was just so excited. This is the first real lead we've had."

"It's okay, honey, I understand, but now suppose we cool down and try to think of the most likely place they could be."

"Do we know where they're planning to get married?"

"We've got a pretty good idea."

"Then we'll start there."

"Wrong. As far as I know, wedding parties don't usually hang around the courthouse to wait out their time."

"You don't know everything."

"I never claimed to know everything," he reminded her. He was thinking fast, trying to figure all the angles, and she wasn't making it any easier, curled up in her seat and leaning toward him until he could smell the soapy warm scent of her body.

"They're in Myrtle," she announced, and he lifted one hand off the steering wheel and let it fall again.

"Carrie!" he exclaimed, exasperated.

"Well, they are! I know they are, Rex. I feel it in my bones."

"What you feel in your bones is incipient arthritis. They say it always gets worse before a storm."

"Bosh! I went with you to Hilton Head, didn't I? You were so certain they'd be there, and you were wrong about that, weren't you? Admit it."

Rex's mood was rapidly deteriorating. His professional ego was on the line, and he wasn't making a very good showing on the personal front, either. Add to that a libido that was cranking out testosterone faster than his body could handle it, and he'd had about all he could take. "You know something, lady? You are irritating, bossy and stubborn. And that's only half of it!"

"The other half being that I was right all along and you were too pigheaded to listen? Tell me something—is it because I'm a woman, and you can't stand being shown up by a woman?"

"No dammit, it's because you're Carrie Lanier!"

Which was so totally irrational that after one instant of stunned silence, she burst out laughing. Half a beat later, he joined in.

"Lord, Carrie, what's happened to us? We never used to set each other off this way."

"Didn't we? Your memory's no better than your disposition."

Driving with the easy skill he'd learned on back roads in souped-up cars, often without benefit of the required documentation, Rex maintained a steady speed, pacing himself with the flow of traffic. "But it was fun, wasn't it? I always knew exactly how to get a rise out of you."

"No more than I did you," she retorted.

"And then we'd both end up laughing. Did I ever tell you that you didn't do a lot for my reputation? The guys all thought I was nuts for hanging around with a kid your age." That wasn't precisely correct, but he didn't think she'd appreciate hearing about all the ribald remarks, even now.

"You did wonders for my ego, but not that much for my reputation. All the girls were sure I was sleeping with you, and they were so jealous!"

"Why didn't you tell them we were just good friends?"

"You think that would've helped?" she scoffed, and he shook his head, grinning at the memory of their unlikely alliance all those years ago.

"Mutt and Jeff," he said.

"Abbott and Costello."

"Romeo and Juliet?" he suggested with a leer, and she laughed again.

"In your dreams!" Actually, it was her own dream, but Carrie didn't think he would care to know that.

But they couldn't avoid the real issue much longer. "Rex, when we find them, do you think we'll be able to talk some sense into their heads before it's too late? Maybe we should try calling around to some of the more likely motels or hotels."

"Like the Mimosa Terrace?"

She nearly rose to the bait, but she knew better now. "It's a starting place."

"They've got until eleven-twenty tomorrow morning. What can they do between now and then that they haven't already done? Why take a chance on spooking them when we can simply cut them off at the pass?"

"You know where to go, then?" Carrie had to admit that it made sense. If they knew they were being followed, they would only move somewhere else. For that matter, she couldn't be all that sure they were even at the Mimosa. Or in Myrtle, come to that. There were dozens of places to sit out a waiting period. Billy would have something to say about it, and somehow, Carrie didn't think the shabby old Mimosa was quite his style.

Any more than it would be Rex's, she reminded herself. It had taken only a single glimpse of Stella's so-called beach cottage to point up the differences between the two families. Billy and Kim might manage to pull it off, but the odds were against it. Against them. Just as they'd been against all the impossible dreams Carrie had harbored in her secret heart all those years ago.

Conversation languished. Rex flexed his shoulders and twisted the dials on the radio, looking for something to keep him alert. He hadn't had a whole lot of sleep last night—or for a lot of nights before that, come to think of it. Stress was a given in his line of work, which was why he'd opted for a couple of weeks alone at the cabin instead of taking Maddie Stone up on her invitation to accompany her to the beach.

Maddie, he thought morosely. There was another thing he was going to have to deal with sooner or later. They'd been drifting along aimlessly for too long, pleasant though the drifting had been. But the last time he'd spent the night at Maddie's place, he'd noticed a *Bride's Magazine* in the breakfast room, which had made him slightly uncomfortable.

"You're awfully quiet," Carrie said softly. "Are you worried?"

"No, just thinking." Evidently there had been a shower shortly before. The tires hummed a monotonous threnody on the wet pavement, adding to the soporific effect of the sultry gray skies.

Rex yawned and muttered an apology.

"Want me to drive?"

"Just talk to me."

"Fight with you, you mean." She laughed, and so did he, but it was subdued laughter. Both were in a subdued frame of mind.

"What do you do for relaxation, Carrie?"

It required a bit of thought, and Carrie took her time.

"Come on now...surely you have some kind of personal life outside the farm," Rex prompted. "Your little girl's practically grown up by now."

"Personal lives are for people with time on their hands. When I have some time, then I'll figure out what to do with it. Leave your name and number with my secretary and I'll have her get back to you when and if it happens." *Take a number and wait, he'd said. God, was it always going to be this way? Was life forever going to be full of traps, waiting to spring the moment she relaxed her guard?*

"That bad, huh?"

"Not really. I happen to enjoy what I do."

"I enjoy what I do, too, but everybody needs a break now and then."

"Oh? Then what do you do for relaxation?"

"Turnabout's fair play, huh? What would you say if I told you that women were my chief form of relaxation?" He was teasing, but with a deeper purpose, one that he was coming to understand more with every passing minute.

"I'd believe you. Your reputation probably hasn't improved all that much since you used to have three dates in a single night."

"Oh, so you heard about that? It was all a misunderstanding. Whatever you've heard, I assure you, it's all a foul plot to discredit the present administration."

"Sure it is," she scoffed. "So tell me, why haven't you ever married?"

He shrugged. "Who knows? There were a couple of near misses, but I reckon I'm just not cut out for marriage." The misses had been a mile wide. The truth was, he'd never found a woman who didn't bore him stiff after a few weeks. No matter how good the sex was, or how brilliant the conversation, sooner or later he always began to feel restless. The amazing thing was that it had taken him all this time to figure out why. "How about you? What about this Don of yours? Was he the only one with the guts to take you on?"

"Oh, there were plenty of takers," Carrie lied blithely. "But none of the others matched my specifications."

"What specs are those? The toothbrush thing?"

"That and a docile temperament. Naturally, they had to agree to allow me to wear the pants in the family. Although I might have eased up on the requirements if I could have found us a good bookkeeper. I hate that part of farming. Or a veterinarian. Lord knows, we could use one of those on permanent retainer. Now I'd probably settle for a good all-round hand who didn't snore and slurp his coffee. If I were looking, that is."

"What about a computer expert?"

"That's an outside option, I suppose. I bought us a small computer year before last, but so far I haven't even had time to learn how to use it, much less transfer all my records. No—I think I'd better hold out for something more practical and less exotic."

"Have you thought about advertising the position?"

"No, but it's an idea. I could post a husband-wanted notice in the local feed and seed stores."

"Wanted, one husband, preferably a sixties or late fifties model, although others will be considered. The best man for the job will receive room, board and the use of a bossy wife."

Carrie chuckled, and Rex did, too. He downshifted to pass a double-tractor trailer, and when a film of dirty spray coated the windshield, he turned on the wipers and the headlights. It was early afternoon, but the sky was growing darker by the minute.

"You know, it would be funny if we ended up in-laws af ter all this time, wouldn't it?" he speculated when the slap click of the wipers had his eyelids sagging again.

Funny? It would be awful! How could she ever hope to keep Jo's paternity from him under those circumstances when they looked like two peas from the same pod? "Is tha what we'd be? Some kind of brother-and-sister-in-law thing once removed?"

"Not too far removed, I hope. Wouldn't you want to be my sister-in-law, Carrie?"

"I don't think we'd be very convincing as family, do you' You're croissant and I'm strictly corn bread. I drive a eight-year-old pickup truck that's rusty from hauling fertil izer. You drive this whatsis thing with leather-covered featherbeds for seats and a full orchestra under your dash board."

"Ouch," he said softly.

"I could go on. You've got one of those fancy car phone: and I use a plain old CB radio. According to Billy, you've got seven hundred and thirteen degrees and I've got a di ploma from Durham County High."

"You've got red hair and mine's only dark brown."

"Black," she countered.

He shrugged. "You've got a rotten temper and I have the disposition of an angel." He pretended to duck, and she giggled. Actually giggled. Carrie didn't remember the last time she'd giggled.

"Did you ever think about what might have happened if we'd stayed in touch?" Rex asked after a while.

Only every day of my life, she wanted to say. "What could've happened? You went off to school, and I stayed home. End of story."

"It didn't have to be that way. It doesn't have to stay that way."

Carrie craned her neck to see the bank of fast-moving clouds coming up from the southwest. "Lord, I hope those clouds dump whatever they're full of before they get up to the state line. Our wheat's going to be ruined if we have to wait much longer to combine it. Do you think—"

"Carrie," he interrupted. "I get over to Durham pretty often." At least he could if there was a reason. "Your place isn't that much farther."

She didn't pretend to misunderstand. That didn't mean she could afford to risk taking him up on whatever he was suggesting. "I don't see much point in it. You've got your interests over in Raleigh, and I—I stay pretty busy."

"Chicken," he said softly.

"Cattle," she corrected.

"We're not finished, lady."

"I know." Carrie flexed her shoulders, leaned her head back against the headrest and closed her eyes. "We still have a wedding to stop."

If she had happened to catch sight of his smile, she would have been even more uneasy than she already was. There was no real hurry, Rex told himself. Now that he'd found her again, he wasn't going to foul things up. Nor was he going to let her get away again, Ralph Lanier or no Ralph Lanier.

Buckshot or no buckshot!

Seven

By midafternoon they were both fit to be tied. Traffic was wall to wall, with more than the usual number of delays. Between that, their growing concerns and the constant threat of storms, Rex and Carrie were both riding on the edge of raw nerves.

"God save me from weekend beach traffic," Rex muttered, after slamming on the brakes behind a convoy of RVs towing boats. There were bicycles tied onto the rear of one of the trailers, and he threatened to buy one on the spot to finish the trip. "It'd be a damned sight quicker than this! Every man, woman and child in three states must be headed to the beach this weekend!"

Carrie was in no better mood. This was their second day on the road, and she hadn't planned to be gone nearly that long. Even one day was too long to be cooped up in a small space with a live volcano. She told him as much, adding, "If you'd just stayed on I-95 a little longer—"

"You want me to go a hundred miles out of my way just to stay on a four-lane highway?"

"It's nowhere near a hundred miles! More like ten if you figure the difference."

"That ten still happens to be in my favor!"

"I doubt it. And anyway, we'd have been there by now if you'd gone my way. But no, you deliberately go out of your way just to find a highway with a lower speed limit!" They'd started out on the Interstate, but then he'd cut over onto another highway that had quickly narrowed down to two lanes.

"It was more direct," he grumbled. "Every fool and his brother must be on the highway today. Damned if there's not a tractor up ahead!"

Carrie was every bit as impatient as he was. "Oh, blast! Wait—I think he's turning off." At any other time, her sympathy would have been with the farmer whose fields the road had bisected. "Anyway, whose fault is it we wasted a whole day? You should've found out about the marriage license yesterday!"

Which was so utterly unjust she was forced to apologize, which didn't do her own frayed nerves any good. "Well, anyway," she muttered, "you should've guessed what they were planning to do."

"Right. Just like I should've guessed— Oh, forget it. We're both tired, and frankly, I'd like to wind up this fiasco before the end of my vacation." He sounded grim and tired and at the end of whatever patience he might once have possessed.

Nor could Carrie blame him. She didn't know why she kept picking fights, except that somewhere in the hinterlands of what passed for her brain, she sensed that it was the safest course.

Five minutes later she was squirming in her seat, leaning forward as if willpower alone could get them through the glut of traffic. "If Billy had a grain of decency, they never would've run off this way, because Kim was brought up to know better."

She waited for him to pick up the gauntlet, and when he didn't, she continued in the same vein. "If he'd had a grain of sense—"

Tanned flesh tightened over angular bones as Rex clenched his jaw. "Carrie, I know you're worried," he began with deceptive gentleness. "And I know that when you're worried, you always fire up that temper of yours to blow off steam. I don't know which one of that pair is responsible for this damned fool stunt, and at this point, I don't give a damn!" Suddenly, to the tune of blaring horns, he swerved over onto a right-of-way and shut off the engine. Fixing her with a heated look, he unsnapped his shoulder harness.

Carrie cowered. "Are you going to—"

That was as far as she got. Reaching over, Rex unsnapped her harness and hauled her bodily out of her seat. His eyes were dark with emotion and his lips were flattened against his white even teeth. "Lady, you've been snapping and sparking like a live wire for two days! I've taken just about all I'm going to take from that smart mouth of yours!"

And then he took something more. Too stunned to avoid him, Carrie felt herself slammed against his hard chest. With no warning, his mouth crushed down on hers, venting all the frustration of two days and fifteen years. This was no gentle exploration, no tentative pressure of flesh against flesh. This was undeclared war!

Without lifting his mouth, Rex growled his displeasure. She wasn't cooperating. She didn't fight him, but neither was she responding. Determined to wrest a reaction her—any reaction at all—he lifted his lips a mere bre from hers and snarled, "Kiss me back, damn you! Open your mouth and kiss me back!"

Either he'd cowed her into obedience or she was slack-jaw scared, and at this point, he didn't much care which. Fifteen years of repressed feelings had suddenly boiled over, and if the timing was all wrong, then that was just tough. He'd run flat out of patience.

Carrie came to her senses just as the universe telescoped into a tiny furnace of desire. She slipped her arms around his neck, and when she opened her mouth and accepted the sweet, familiar taste of him—met the thrust of his tongue with a tentative thrust of her own, neither of them noticed the cars roaring past, some jeering, some cheering. They were in a world of their own.

For Rex, that world began and ended with this one small woman. She had burrowed under his skin all those years ago and made herself so much a part of him that he hadn't even realized she was there, but he knew it now. And God help him, she was going to know it, too!

There was a dazed look in Carrie's dark eyes when Rex finally lifted his head. Her swollen lips were still parted. He swore softly, wondering just when he'd finally lost it. Even in the old days he would have had better sense than to pull a stunt like this. And not just because it was broad daylight and the entire population of South Carolina was streaming past a few feet away.

Feeling as if he had barely escaped a quicksand bog, he smoothed a wild curl off her face. "That's all that's saving you, you know," he told her, nodding to the busy highway a few feet away.

"Am I saved?" Carrie whispered. Utterly shattered, she lay in his arms and willed her head to stop spinning.

"Do you want to be saved?"

One corner of her lips quirked upward. "Is this a revival meeting?"

"I'm not sure. I thought it was bells I was hearing, but maybe it's gospel music."

She laughed breathlessly. "I think it's something a little racier than that. You left the radio on."

From the four speakers came a fast-paced rundown on the upcoming speed trials at Darlington Speedway. Rex switched off the sound, and gradually a sense of time and place returned. Self-consciously, Carrie pulled away, and Rex braced both hands on the steering wheel to keep from reaching for her again. "Sorry," he said gruffly. "I didn't mean to jump you like that, but it was the quickest way I could think of to shut you up."

Carrie seemed to shrink before his eyes. "Next time, just try telling me to be quiet. I can take a hint."

He cursed himself for a clumsy fool. He hadn't meant it that way. He didn't know what he *had* meant, but he'd never meant to hurt her. Again. "You were in a transmitting mode, not a receiving mode."

Waiting for a lull in traffic, he pulled back onto the highway, being doubly cautious because he was still feeling raw. It was that extra awareness that probably saved their lives a few minutes later.

Rex was glancing at his side mirror when he saw it. Out of the leaden sky, the thing was coming straight for them, dipping and dancing across the treetops.

"Jesus!" He breathed, leaning on the horn even as he swerved back off the highway. Shouting for Carrie to hit the dirt, he shoved open his door and was around to hers before she could strip off her harness.

He tore it off, dragging her out of the car. "Twister! Dive for the ditch!"

Others had seen it by now. Horns were blaring, brakes were screeching. Some drivers picked up speed in an effort to outrun the thing, others swerved to the side, and still others stopped dead in the road.

Carrie stood frozen in her tracks, her hair blowing around her face. As the sound of a freight train bore down on them, Rex tackled her, hurtling them both into the shallow depression beside the road. He covered her with his body, neither of them breathing, while all hell roared overhead.

A lifetime later, he eased his weight off her body. Carrie could feel his heart pounding a mile a minute. That meant he was alive . . . didn't it? Evidently, so was she.

Suddenly it was swelteringly hot. She was wringing wet, vaguely aware of something warm and sticky under her back. She squinched her eyes shut, fearful of what she might see.

"Carrie? Sweetheart, it's over. Open your eyes."

She did, one at a time. And then she sniffed. "What smells so awful? Rex, was that really . . . what I think it was?"

"A tornado? If it wasn't, I'm going to feel pretty damned foolish after throwing you into a drainage ditch and diving in on top of you. Are you okay? Did I break anything?'

"Nothing of mine, at least. I'm only slightly squashed. How about you?"

"All parts seem to be in working order. Honey, you're not only squashed, you're a real mess. It's this ditch we're in that stinks."

He helped her to stand, and together they cleaned her off as best they could. Rex winced as he flexed his elbows, and Carrie insisted on examining them. They were muddy and scraped raw, but one glance around was enough to tell them that they'd both got off easy.

Vehicles were scattered like jackstraws. A boat trailer had come unhitched and was lying on its side, its cargo splintered by a pine tree. The tree itself was broken off about halfway up, as were some dozen or so others. A sheet of twisted metal dangled from the top of a tractor trailer, and there was an aluminum beach chair wrapped around a telephone pole. As far as Rex could tell, there was no more serious damage than that. At least not in their immediate vicinity.

"That was a close call," Carrie whispered.

"God knows what would have happened if the thing had dipped instead of skipped at this particular spot. Come on, let's get out of here."

Seven No Vacancy signs later Rex pulled into one of the larger chain motels and shut off the engine. Lifting his hands from the steering wheel, he was not particularly surprised to see they were shaking—not to mention muddy and bloody. "Wait here, honey. If this one's full-up, too, I'm going to rent the damned lobby!"

There was no question of separate rooms. Neither of them wanted to be alone. Carrie followed him with her eyes as he disappeared through the double glass doors. She felt like running after him, not wanting to be left alone even for a moment, but her whole backside was muddy. They'd scraped off all they could, from her hair, her skin and her clothes, but she was still far from presentable.

Besides, she wasn't sure her legs would support her.

It had taken them almost two hours to get this far, dodging around stalled vehicles, helping out along the way wherever help was needed. Rex's muscular strength had come in handy more than once, but watching him rock a terrified child in his arms and talk a six-year-old out of hysterics while Carrie helped the mother collect their scattered clothing, had come as a surprise.

Although it shouldn't have. The Rex she remembered from the early years had comforted her more than once, with an insight far beyond his meager years.

Carrie was still running on adrenaline, and she suspected Rex was, too. Only now was it beginning to sink in on her just how close they'd both come to being seriously injured. Or worse.

Power. Never in all her life had she witnessed such a devastating display of sheer, awesome power! At five-foot-two, she had never felt particularly impressive, but in all her thirty years, she had never felt quite so small, so terrifyingly helpless. If Rex hadn't been there . . .

But he had. He had known just what to do and had done it instantly. Because of him, they were safe. Dirty and shaken, but blessedly safe!

Suddenly, her face crumpled and she started to cry.

"Hey, come on now, sweetheart, don't fall apart on me now," Rex said, slipping in beside her. He covered both her hands with one of his own and watched helplessly while she sat staring straight in front of her, tears streaming down her face.

And then he started the car and drove around to the room he'd booked, wondering if crying wasn't the best way to get it all out. If he thought it would help, he might shed a few tears himself. A hundred years from now, should he live so long, Rex knew he would still remember the way she had looked standing there beside the road, her eyes enormous in a pale, luminous face, her flaming hair highlighted against that monstrous sky. In that one split second, Rex had known she was the beginning and the end of his life.

"This is getting to be a habit," he said with a laugh that didn't quite come off as he let them both into the spacious room.

There was no pretense of modesty. They'd come too far for that. They were both filthy, bloody and shaken, and Carrie eased her ruined sandals off her feet and then slipped off her new skirt before dropping into one of the chairs. She had lost an earring. Now she tossed its pink plastic mate into the trash. They'd been sheer bravado, anyway, and she'd just learned that bravado was a pitifully inadequate defense.

Rex went outside and returned a moment later with his overnight bag. "I'm fresh out of underwear, but I can let you have my bathing trunks and a pair of socks." He glanced down at the knees of his khakis and frowned. "Looks like one of us is going to have to hit the mall."

"You're the cleanest. Next time, I get to be on top." She grimaced at her own double entendre, but Rex let it pass without comment, glad to see the color come flooding back to her face.

"I knew it. You just don't trust me to shop for you, do you?'

"I don't have much choice, unless I wrap up in the sheet and go as a ghost."

"Or a Roman. Come on, help me clean up a bit first, and I'll go find us both a change of clothes, some first-aid supplies and some food. Got any requests?"

She managed a weak smile. "Cheap, something that doesn't sting, and lots of it, respectively speaking."

Rex removed his shirt, and Carrie, wearing her half-slip and her muddy blouse, helped him sponge off his hands, elbows and the knees of his khakis. Fighting the familiar urge to curl up in his powerful arms and shut out the rest of the world, she surveyed the damage. "I guess it's not quite as bad as it looks, as long as you remember to douse on a good antiseptic. Once it starts healing, it's going to hurt like the dickens every time you flex your elbows, though." She spoke with the authority of a mother whose child had scraped everything scrapable in the process of growing up.

"I'll survive." The feel of her callused little hands moving over his body was having a far greater effect on him than all his scrapes and bruises put together. He didn't think an antiseptic would do much for that particular problem.

"We both will, thanks to you. I didn't even thank you," she whispered. The hands on his arm grew still for a moment, and Rex cursed himself silently for reminding her of what could have happened.

Snatching his shirt off the doorknob, he rammed his arms in the sleeves. "Forget it. Just finish up in the bathroom before I get back, will you? Because I plan to tie up that tub for at least an hour."

Rex was just now beginning to realize how sore he was all over. He must have clenched every muscle in his body in the few seconds between spotting the funnel and hitting the ditch. "Sorry, honey. I didn't mean to snap at you. Look, I'm gone, okay? Be back in an hour or so. I seem to remember passing some kind of shopping center a few miles back."

Carrie followed him to the door, not wanting to be alone but unwilling to admit it. "Don't you need to know my size?"

His eyes were bleak, but he smiled. "Trust me, okay?"

He was back before she was quite steady. With a basket of courtesy toiletries, Carrie had enjoyed the luxury of shampooing her hair, conditioning it and smoothing body lotion all over her aching muscles. Lineament would probably have been more effective, but she didn't happen to have any.

Having washed her underwear and twisted it in a towel, she had just draped the pieces over the clothes rack when Rex returned. He let himself in, tossed several large parcels on the bed and placed another one on the round table beside the window.

Carrie, draped in a towel, leaped for the bed and dragged the sheet over her before reaching for the nearest sack.

"I got us barbecue plates, that okay by you?"

"Sounds wonderful!" Still somewhat shaken, but feeling considerably better after her bath, she dipped into the sack and pulled out a pair of men's briefs. Navy blue. "Oops! Sorry."

"Help yourself if you think they'll fit." Rex grinned, picturing her shapely little derriere in his underwear.

Carrie stuffed them back into the bag and reached for one of the others. "I'm almost afraid to see what you picked out for me. Are the receipts insides?"

"Forget the receipts. Let's eat first and then you can tell me how much you admire my taste in women's clothing."

"Okay, we'll eat first, but I don't intend to forget anything. I'm keeping a careful account of every cent I owe you, and I promise you I'll repay every penny."

Rex had been sitting in one of the two straight chairs, tilting it back off the floor. Now the front legs came down with a muffled thud, and he glowered. "Would you climb off your high horse, lady? I'm not threatening your independence. You can pay me back later if you insist on it. It's not important. Now, do you want to eat this stuff before it congeals, or do you want to pick another fight?"

Her chin wobbled, but she recovered almost immediately. Which was probably just as well. They both needed food, and if he'd touched her then, he couldn't have guaranteed they'd get any dinner, and maybe not any breakfast, either.

Rex waded through nearly half his barbecue plate. Carrie managed to get down a few bites. It looked delectable. It smelled wonderful, but her appetite seemed to have fled.

"What's the matter, don't you like it?" Rex asked. He was sprawled out in the chair, while Carrie still sat cross-legged on the bed.

"I guess maybe I wasn't as hungry as I thought." She closed the box and held it out to him. Her hand was trembling.

"Why don't you try on what I brought you while I go shower, and then we'll play doctor?" When her auburn eyebrows shot up, he indicated the small white sack on the table. "First-aid stuff."

Carrie regained her composure enough to say, "There's still a few drops of shampoo left. Fortunately, you don't have nearly as much hair as you used to."

"The least of my worries," he told her, and then with a wicked grin, he disappeared into the bathroom.

Carrie dumped the remaining parcels onto the bed. By the time she took inventory, she was torn between laughter and indignation. What did he think she was, for goodness' sake! Black *lace?* She never worn black lace drawers in her entire life. The matching bra was a size too small, but it would do—32 D-cups weren't always easy to find.

There were two sets of underwear, one black, the other taupe, and a nightgown that was made like a choir robe, except that few choir robes came in orchid chiffon, with a lace panel down the front. There were two pairs of shoes— one pair of white high-heeled sandals and a pair of navy blue sneakers, both the right size. There was also a sundress of yellow-and-white cotton that looked not only smart, but suspiciously expensive. A pair of blue-and-white flowered slacks and a navy silk blouse—genuine silk, not polyester—completed the lot.

"Oh, Rex," Carrie whispered, surveying it all. "It's easy to see what kind of women you're used to dressing."

Not one single item would she have chosen for herself. Well . . . maybe the navy blue sneakers. But the rest? They were totally impractical, and if she were any judge of quality, none of them had come cheap. At this rate, she'd be in hock to the man for the next forty years!

By the time Rex emerged from the bathroom in a cloud of fragrant steam, Carrie was wearing her voluminous nightgown over the taupe underwear. To keep it from tripping her up, she had caught it up at the waist with the tooled leather belt she wore with her jeans. In lieu of slippers, she had put on her new navy sneakers, and she had to laugh at the look on his face when he saw her.

"Somehow that's not quite the way I pictured you when I picked out that nightgown."

"I can imagine what you pictured," she said, allowing amusement to win out over jealousy. With his looks and reputation, he had probably seen more women in nightgowns—and out of them—than most men see in a lifetime. "Pajamas would've made more sense. I could've rolled up the legs."

She tried to avoid looking at him, but it was almost impossible. He was wearing a fresh pair of khakis. Other than that, he was bare. The pattern of dark hair that swirled across the broad expanse of his chest drew her eyes like a magnet, and she followed it as it veed down toward his waist. He was broader, deeper in the chest, but just as lean as ever. He hadn't yet removed his belt from his old khakis, and either the clip at the top of his new slacks had come open, or he hadn't bothered to fasten it. Either way, the effect was as devastating as any tornado.

"Carrie? You feeling all right? What about the rest of the stuff? Does it fit?"

"It's just fine." She hadn't even tried on the dress, and she wasn't about to tell him he was one size off on the bra. "The shoes are perfect, but I almost never wear high heels."

"What about your boots?"

"Oh, those? I need the heels for—um, fence climbing," she said, turning away to gather up the clothing scattered across the bed. The truth was, the boots were her one vanity. She dressed like a farmhand and looked like a farmhand because she *was* a farmhand. But nobody ever said all farmhands had to wear hobnail boots.

"Sorry if I screwed up. It was a small shopping center," Rex said gruffly. "I couldn't see my elbows, but my hands checked out okay after I got 'em clean."

Carrie nodded toward the bathroom, feeling anything but maternal. "I'd better take a look. They were pretty bloody."

He stepped inside the claustrophobic room and she followed him. It was still steamy, still redolent of soap and after-shave and toothpaste.

"You don't have to do this if you don't want to," he said, watching her closely. "I heal quickly."

"You sound just like Jo." She reached for his arm. "Turn toward the light so I can see what you've done to yourself," she said, positioning him to her liking.

He'd bought elastic gauze and two different kinds of antiseptic. Working together, they managed to anoint his elbows. She bandaged them both, but his hands required only a dab of antiseptic.

Then it was her turn. "What about that place where the blackberry cane caught you when we were climbing out of the ditch?"

She'd almost forgotten it. Rex insisted on looking it over, and she braced herself on the towel rack while he lifted her left leg to examine her calf.

"Use the stuff in the tube, not that other—*ouch!*"

"Too late. What about any bruises you got when I piled in on top of you? Your back? Your shoulders? Your... ah..." His voice sounded as if it had been strained through burlap.

"I never bruise."

He lowered her leg gently and reached for her shoulders, turning her to face him. "Then I guess that about does it." His eyes moved over her face, coming to rest on her mouth.

Was it possible to catch a fever from a tornado? Carrie wondered. She watched his eyes go from silver to pewter and couldn't have looked away if her life depended on it.

"Rex, I—"

"Carrie, if—"

"You first," she whispered.

He took a deep breath and then he drew her deliberately into his arms, crushing her against his naked chest.

She came willingly, and Rex knew then that it was going to happen. "Carrie," he whispered hoarsely, "I want to make love to you. If you don't want it, you'd better say so now, because you won't get a second chance."

But this *is* my second chance. The thought etched itself in her consciousness as she met him halfway, drawn by a force more powerful than any tornado, a force that had been growing ever since he'd left her aching, angry and pregnant, without a word of hope, or love, or even of goodbye.

Rex groaned. She'd been beautiful at fifteen. At thirty, she was magnificent. All fire and passion, strength and softness. He held her too tightly, but she didn't try to get away. Being Carrie, she would always give as much as she took. And Rex took everything. Took it all and wanted more. By the time the kiss ended, he had slipped her gown over her shoulders and it drooped from her waist, held there by the leather belt.

Breathing hard, he removed her bra and then he held her away. "I could never get enough of looking at you," he whispered shakily, still reeling from a kiss that had started out explosively and escalated from there. Lifting her hands, he placed them on his chest and said, "I haven't forgotten a single time, Carrie—tell me you haven't, either."

Carrie's fingers trailed down his resilient flesh, savoring the heat of him, the strength, the exciting texture of silken skin and wiry hair. Seeing her own callused hands, the nails clipped off short and innocent of polish, she wished she could be different for him—wished she could be better, more beautiful, more experienced. "Rex, why didn't you—" She'd been going to say, why didn't you take me with you? Foolish question.

But he understood. "Darling, you were fifteen. I couldn't have taken care of you. They'd have found us and taken you away from me."

"I wouldn't have let them."

"You wouldn't have had a choice. Anyway, it wouldn't have worked, Carrie, don't you understand? It would've been a big mistake, sweetheart. We both know I've made more mistakes than I can count, but that one wouldn't have affected just me. I just couldn't risk it for you. What if you'd gotten pregnant? Think about your sister, the way you feel about the risks she's taking with Billy. She's three years older than you were then, and those three years are crucial in a girl's life."

Carrie wanted to laugh. She wanted to cry. She wanted to tell him the truth, but didn't dare. "You're such an expert on young girls' lives?"

"You'd better believe it," he replied, a rueful smile twisting his lips. "I was the acknowledged authority on all matters female in my senior year, don't forget. I didn't want you to grow up and start resenting, or even regretting, any decisions we'd made when we were too young to know better."

She looked up, her face flushed and her eyes suspiciously bright. "I can't believe what I'm hearing. Are you sure we're talking about the same Rex Ryder, the toughest, wildest boy in the senior class?"

"We're talking about Rex Ryder, who learned most of life's lessons the hard way." And too late, he could have added, but didn't. Something dark and hard flickered briefly in his eyes as he looked at her, clutching that ridiculous orchid gown over her chest, and Rex felt the past slip away as if it had never been.

Carrie backed away, suddenly nervous. It had been so long since she'd made love with a man. Fifteen years, to be exact. With Don, it had been sex, never love. And they'd both known the difference.

Eight

Against his will, Rex had to smile at the ninety-nine pounds of sheer spunk and spirit, clad in leather-belted orchid chiffon and navy sneakers, with a wild crop of red hair drying in tangled curls around her small pale face. "Don't think you can back out now. You'd dare the devil in his own parlor, wouldn't you?" he demanded softly.

Her small store of courage seeping away, Carrie grabbed up another fistful of nightgown and tried to make it cover more of her. "I think I just did."

"I think you just did, too, sweetheart. Come here."

"There's, um...something I think you should know. Maybe we'd better talk some more."

"We've already talked, and where has it gotten us? No woman has ever put me through as many emotional wringers as you have, lady. Either you come over here, or I'll go over there."

Matching words with action, he crossed to where she hovered near the foot of one of the room's two double beds. Carrie backed up two steps for every one of his, coming to a halt only when she felt the nightstand at her back. "Rex," she warned.

"Chicken?"

"I've changed my mind."

"Why?" He didn't push her. He didn't want her scrambling over the bed with that stupid nightgown flapping around her feet. They'd both suffered enough physical damage for one day.

"Look, maybe this is another mistake."

"It doesn't feel like a mistake to me." His eyes gleamed, and he reached out and finished unbuckling her belt. It fell to the floor.

"Couldn't we just . . . ah, talk some more?"

"When did talking ever get us anything but trouble?"

"Don't forget Kim and Billy," she said in a defensive rush of words. Rex had paced her every step until she was practically sitting on top of the nightstand. He reached around her and rescued the phone before it crashed to the floor, and then braced his arms against the wall on either side of her, blocking her escape.

"Forget Kim and Billy."

"How can I forget them? They're the reason we're here!"

Eyes gleaming in the muted light, Rex smiled at her. "Are they?"

"This is crazy! Just because we ran into each other again after so long—just because we happen to get caught in a—"

Capturing her chin, Rex tilted her face and silenced her in the most efficient way he knew. Fiercely at first, and then more gently as she began to melt in his arms—using skills acquired over a wide, if not particularly deep, career as a lover of women—he seduced her with kisses until she was practically sobbing in his arms. "You were saying?" he prompted. Something shifted imperceptibly in his expression as he watched her struggle to compose herself.

"Rex, we can't just—"

He closed her mouth with a finger. "We can. This is our time, Carrie. Yours and mine. It was a long time coming."

When he lifted her hands from her gown and allowed it to slither to the floor, she didn't resist. Slowly, lovingly, he smoothed the lacy pants down over her hips, catching his breath at the sheer feminine perfection revealed there. Maturity had only enhanced it. With hands that were far from steady, he tackled the fastening of the scrap of taupe lace that clung to the tips of her breasts.

When that fell, he stepped back. His eyes gleamed over her, lingering on her full, creamy breasts with their small pink tips, on the waist that looked even tinier by comparison. On the rounded swell of her hips and the fiery thicket that guarded her feminine secrets.

Like a man coming out of a long trance, Rex shook his head, then sat her down on the bed, where he removed the new canvas sneakers. Measuring one bare foot against the palm of his hand, he said, "This is how I knew your size. I've never forgotten."

The riverside again, he mused. How could one fleeting moment in time have such a profound effect on a man's life?

Quickly, he removed the rest of his clothing, touched that she didn't look away. Neither bold nor shy, she was simply...Carrie. In the rather superficial way of teenagers, he had always known that there were depths behind the quick temper, the equally quick wit. Older now, he was more certain than ever that he'd been right.

Pressing her onto the bed, he switched off the bedside light, leaving only one small lamp on the far side of the room. Sealed into an intimate cocoon of near darkness, he came down beside her.

"I'm not going to rush you, Carrie." He waited, watching, giving her time to change her mind. Praying she wouldn't. And then, when she didn't, he deliberately angled his face over hers.

Carrie left her eyes open until the very last instant. This was Rex. Not a memory. Not a dream. Not a dated photograph in an old high school annual, but Rex in the flesh. She met him halfway, and they kissed, gently at first, and then more fiercely. Driven by desperate need, two pairs of hands moved urgently, exploring, caressing, remembering. Always before they'd been impatient, lacking the time and wisdom to savor their brief stolen moments.

This time, Rex wanted to give her everything in his power to give, but he was rapidly reaching the limits of his control. Scratches, scrapes and bruises were forgotten as they touched, embraced, and then leaned back to stare at each other, bemused.

"What have you done to me?" he marveled softly.

All I've done is love you forever, Carrie wanted to tell him, but didn't quite dare. "No more than you've done to me," she whispered.

His angular jaw, freshly shaven, dragged over her cheeks as he sought her mouth again. While his hands moved over her burning body, inciting riots wherever they touched, his tongue dueled skillfully with hers. Drowning in her own senses, Carrie traced the familiar planes of his body, from the pelt on his chest, down his rigid abdomen, and beyond.

"Sweetheart, you don't know what you're doing to me." He captured her hand and pressed it against his hardened flesh, and then dragged it away again. "Short fuse," he gasped. "Some things haven't changed."

Then it was her turn to gasp. When he buried his face in her lush breasts and began to suckle, she went quietly out of her mind. Her fingers raked through his hair, and she moaned softly. By the time he lifted his head she was writhing beneath him.

Rex braced his weight on his arms, trying vainly to hide the fact that he was trembling. "Darling, I don't want to rush you, but—"

"Rush me. Oh, please, rush me! If you don't, I'll die."

He needed no second urging. Turning away, he reached for his wallet and Carrie wondered if he always carried protection or if he'd bought it when he'd stopped at the drugstore, just in case.

It didn't matter. She almost wished he didn't have it, because the thought of having his child growing inside her again was suddenly infinitely desirable.

Are you out of your mind? The last thing you need is for history to repeat itself!

Thank goodness she was old enough to know better now. But then he touched her in such a way that the last shred of rational thought fizzled out like spent fireworks. She caught his hand. "Rex," she whispered breathlessly.

"Close your eyes. Let me make you bloom, sweetheart."

And bloom she did, amidst rainbows, shooting stars and soft explosions that rocked her to her very roots. "I can't— Oh, please," she whispered urgently as she tugged on his shoulders. "I can't *stand* any more!"

Rex waited no longer. He'd wanted to make it last, wanted to make it unforgettable for her, but he wasn't made of stone. At least, not all over.

Gently probing the entrance to her heated flesh, he cautioned himself to take it slowly, not to charge in like a rutting bull. But he'd waited too long. "Ahhh, Carrie..." And then she wrapped her sweet legs around him, and he was lost.

A long time later, Rex lifted his head from the pillow and studied the face beside his own. She was sleeping ... wasn't she? Her eyes were closed, her lids faintly shadowed. Her mouth was slightly parted, her lips swollen, and there was a place on her shoulder where he'd nipped her too hard.

Carrie. His own sweet Carrie. With a cold fierceness, he thought of the man who had given her a child. That privilege should have belonged to him!

Sunshine slanted across the foot of the bed when Carrie opened her eyes. At first she couldn't think where she was, and why she was so sore, but then it came back to her. The tornado.

Her eyes widened. No, not the tornado. Rex!

With a guilty flush, she glanced at the pillow beside her. It bore a faint indentation, but that was all. Leaning forward, she peered around to see if the bathroom door was shut, but it was standing open.

Could she have dreamed the whole thing?

No. She simply didn't have the capacity to dream something like that.

But where was he? Surely he wouldn't have? ...

Not after—

Just before pragmatism gave way to panic, the door opened and Rex stepped inside, bearing two covered trays. "This is getting to be a habit, lady. Next time it's my turn to have breakfast in bed."

He smiled, but there was a wary look in his eyes, as if he wasn't quite certain of his reception.

Carrie leaped on the topic to keep from plunging into something she wasn't yet ready to confront. "I hope that's not a Danish," she said, her voice soft with morning huskiness. "I never eat sweets for breakfast."

"Me either. If I did, you'd be in danger."

Rex devoured her with his eyes, feeling an awkwardness he hadn't felt with a woman since he was sixteen. He'd tried to cover with a joke, but neither of them was in a joking mood. "Want me to hand you a shirt?" he asked gruffly. "It's chilly in here." She was naked, still flushed from sleep, and he was fully clothed. At this moment he wanted nothing more than to peel off his clothes and climb back into that rumpled bed, but he didn't dare.

He tossed her the navy silk blouse, and she rammed her fists into the sleeves and buttoned it up, one hole out of phase. "I should've bought you a bathrobe while I was at it."

"No, you shouldn't, I never wear them." She avoided meeting his eyes.

"Hey, I got us bacon, scrambles, hash browns and biscuits, okay?" he announced with forced cheerfulness.

"I can't eat until I've washed my face," she mumbled, scurrying into the bathroom. Her shirttail wasn't quite long enough for modesty, but Rex had an idea she wasn't in the mood for any bottom-line jokes.

He told himself that he could afford to be patient. During the time it had taken him to locate the motel's restaurant and make his way through the breakfast buffet, he had done some thinking. The conclusions he'd reached, if they proved out, were pretty encouraging.

First of all, she'd been just as eager as he'd been last night. There was no way he could have been wrong about that. Rex had known passionate women, lukewarm women and cold ones who pretended enjoyment for reasons of their own. Carrie was in a class by herself. The temper should've tipped him off. She had more than enough fire to spare, and when she gave, she gave wholeheartedly, the same way she did everything else.

What they needed was a wide slice of privacy and no interruptions. Unfortunately, that was a luxury that was going to have to wait. First, they were going to have to deal with Billy and Kim. At this point, that young pair was the last thing on his mind, but he knew Carrie was worried. And once they got around to sorting out their own affairs, he didn't want her distracted.

Forty-five minutes later, they were back on the road. Rex tried to concentrate on the mission at hand, but all he could think of was that he'd like to be in their place. With Carrie. With a lifetime ahead of them to explore all the realms— mental, spiritual, emotional and physical.

Although at the moment, he had to confess that the physical took precedence over all the rest.

Carrie was edgy. She wouldn't quite look him in the eye, and whenever he tried to talk about what had happened, she changed the subject, only to fall silent a few moments later.

Rex allowed her to get away with it. For now. They had a four-hour drive ahead of them, and if Kim and Billy didn't turn up where he'd predicted they would, he had an idea Miss Carrie was going to be demanding his head served up on a platter.

Oddly enough, he found that he missed her bickering. He'd always got a kick out of it, knowing that she cooled off as quickly as she flared up. Besides, being this close to her wasn't exactly conducive to rational thought.

He shifted his position, switched on the radio and then switched it off again. He adjusted the visor, opened the sunroof and then wiped one damp palm after the other on his pants legs.

Whew! Unless he got his imagination back under control, he was going to need a fire extinguisher!

In lieu of that, he forced himself to go through the step-by-step process of finding the evidence needed to convict in his most recent case. The trail had been tedious, clever and quirky as a left-handed corkscrew. He'd been ready to give up more than once, but he'd stuck it out. And in the end, he had triumphed, thanks to a mix of one part brilliant deduction, one part sheer luck, and ninety-eight parts pure drudgery.

But that case was finished, the next one wasn't even on his desk yet, and there was nothing to keep his mind off Carrie Lanier.

What was he going to do about her?

What did he *want* to do about her?

The answer to the second question was easy. He wanted to take her to bed again. And again and again. And then he wanted to tie her up so securely that she wouldn't give a sweet damn who ran her father's farm.

"Carrie—"

"Rex, what time is it? I forgot to wind my watch last night."

They had just crossed the I-95 and picked up Highway 20 toward Columbia. Sunday-morning traffic was relatively light. Rex settled into a comfortable rate of speed and glanced at his watch. "Nine twenty-two. Carrie, how long do you plan to go on pretending that last night never happened?"

So much for timing. "I don't know what you mean."

He could almost hear her defenses clicking into place. "You know what I mean, all right. One thing I never figured you for was a coward." Thus lighting her fuse, Rex waited. It took her all of thirty seconds to go off.

"You haven't changed one bit, have you? You always did have trouble with priorities. In case you've forgotten, we've got less than two hours to get to this marriage place you're talking about before Kim wrecks her whole life, and you want to talk about your—your exploits!''

Amused, he played along. "My *exploits?* Honey, you flatter me. I haven't had time for a decent exploit in months.''

"You know what I'm talking about,'' she muttered. "Your conquests.''

"Ah, so we're talking about conquests. That's hardly the same thing as exploits.'' He changed lanes as a semi rolled off the exit without slowing up. "Did you have any particular conquest in mind, or are we speaking generally?''

Her hands chopped the air with an impatient gesture, and without even seeing them, Rex knew her eyes would be flashing dark fire. "Carrie, Carrie, why do I keep baiting you?''

She sighed. "How do I know? Maybe because you enjoy seeing me rise to the bait.''

"I enjoy seeing you, period. I enjoy sparring with you, I enjoy traveling with you—but most of all, I enjoy making love with you.'' He waited a moment before going on. "If you care to return the compliment, I'm all ears.''

Carrie scowled at his right ear. It wasn't small, nor was it too large. It was . . . perfect. His hair, black in some lights, dark brown in others, barely brushed it, as if he were about a week late getting it cut. "All right, me too,'' she said grudgingly, and he pretended not to understand.

"You enjoy making love?''

"I enjoy fighting with you! I enjoy—at least I don't mind traveling with you.''

"And the rest of it?'' he taunted gently.

"Oh, shut up!''

"What's the matter, darling? Too early in the day for romance?''

With the redhead's emotional barometer, her face went from pale peach to hot-pink, and Rex's taunting chuckle turned into a tender smile. He hoped the day never came when he couldn't bring the color rushing to her cheeks.

She'd bought herself a reprieve. Rex turned on the radio and found a country music station. Waylon Jennings might sing about love and sex and broken dreams on a summer Sunday morning, but Rex decided he'd do better to put things on hold. In a few hours they should be able to wind up this business with the kids, and then he could concentrate on more important issues.

"I figure we've got about a half hour's lead time," he said.

"*If* you were right about where they were headed."

"This little town I told you about—Lester? It's supposed to be the marriage capital around these parts. The license was taken out in Lester County, so I figure it's a pretty safe bet that's where they're headed."

"And if you're wrong? What'll we do then?"

He grinned without looking around. "We'll think of something."

Carrie sighed heavily, and Rex tried to focus his attention on driving. It was damned near impossible. If she had any idea what one of those bosom-heaving sighs of hers did to his good intentions, she might not be sitting there quite so calmly.

They arrived in the small town with a good twenty minutes to spare, and Rex pulled into a service station. While Carrie used the ladies' room, Rex corralled the only attendant on duty.

"Say a couple wanted to get married around here—where would they be likely to go?'

The attendant wiped off his wrench on a pair of greasy coveralls, laid it carefully on a filthy, littered shelf and scratched the side of his bulbous nose. "'Pends on whether they're Baptists, Meth'dists or Fruitful Lifers. 'Course, there's some that gets married at home."

"Say they're from out of town," Rex offered impatiently.

"In that case, I reckon they'd prob'ly go down to Little Joe's place."

"How far?" Rex glanced at his watch and the man grinned knowingly.

"Just foller this road, hang a left at the stop light, another left at the Moose Lodge and keep on going about three, four miles. It's on the right—you can't miss it. Big sign out front and a gravel parking lot on the side."

Rex slipped a bill from his wallet and the man palmed it with the deftness of a master magician. "That your woman in the car? Looks like you got yourself a real sweet deal there, mister. Me, I wouldn't even care if she could'n cook, but if she can, you got it made in the shade."

Heat radiated up from the oil-stained concrete and bounced off the brick walls as Rex strode back to where Carrie waited. Climbing inside, he shut the overhead flap and switched on the air conditioner. "You want something cold to drink from the machine?"

"I can wait. Did you find out anything?"

"Yeah. I found out that if you can cook, too, I've got it made in the shade. Whatever that means."

Little Joe's World Famous Wedding Parlor was not hard to find. In the first place, the building itself was bright yellow with freshly painted white trim. There was a sign out front that was almost as big as the building itself, and as if that weren't enough, a bouquet of tired Mylar balloons attached to one corner of the sign dipped lazily in the heated air whenever a car passed.

"Rex," Carrie began, but he'd already seen it. There was a red Mustang parked behind the wedding parlor between a yellow pickup truck and a gleaming, high-finned black Cadillac.

"That's Billy's. Let's go."

Nine

It was like an assembly line. If Rex had thought about it, he might have been prepared, but his mind was on something else. He opened the front door to be greeted by a blast of scented, frigid air and an electronic version of the traditional wedding march.

"Damn," he muttered. "Why couldn't they have—"

That was as far as he got before a well-cushioned woman in a pink flowered dress jammed a bouquet of fake flowers into Carrie's hand at the same time some jerk in a mortician's suit shoved Rex's arms into a black coat, complete with pink plastic carnation in the buttonhole. Handed a collar with black tie attached and asked to put it on, Rex was still standing there like a poleaxed steer when some skinny kid with a Polaroid started snapping pictures.

Five minutes later, having explained that they were family, not victims, they were ushered into a painfully pink waiting room.

Now, still scowling, Rex brushed the rice from his hair and tried not to inhale too deeply of the heavily scented air. Kimberly Ann Lanier, he concluded, was a remarkably pretty girl, even when she was sulking. By ordinary standards she was probably prettier than her older sister. But then Carrie wasn't ordinary, in any sense of the word. Never had been.

He knew an unexpected feeling of loss for all the years in her life he had missed. Carrie at eighteen would have been something to behold. All that spit and sizzle, just beginning to be tempered by maturity. No wonder she had been snatched up. But what had that fool—what was his name, Don? What had he been thinking of to let her get away?

Forcing his attention to the task at hand, he said, "Don't you two think you might do better to give it a little more time?"

"We already gave it time." Billy's initial belligerence had quickly given way to sullenness. "We've been planning this since February."

"Since February!" Carrie exclaimed. "Kimberly—"

Rex laid his hand on her arm. They had decided before-hand that he would tackle them first, as Carrie was inclined to overheat.

"That long, hmm? Then I reckon you've pretty well worked out all the kinks by now."

"Damn right we have," Billy muttered. He was trying to look tough, but with that lick-spit-polished face of his, it was a lost cause.

Rex leaned back in the pink velvet love seat. They were using the parlor provided as a waiting room, and at the moment, they had it to themselves. "Glad to hear it. Was your mother very upset at losing you? Commuting to college is one thing, but moving out of her nest to start your own is something else."

Billy frowned. "Moving out?"

"Well, sure . . . unless Kim particularly wants to live with her mother-in-law. Personally, I don't think that's such a good idea. A young couple just starting out needs a lot of privacy."

Knowing Stella, Rex mused, the poor girl would be crying by the end of the first day and gone by the end of the second. "But then," he continued, "you've probably already figured that out for yourself. If you haven't found anything yet, I know of a pretty decent subdivision not too far out of town. Friend of mine designed the houses. They're small, but not bad, considering the price range. The down payment shouldn't be more than twenty grand, but if you could swing thirty, the monthly payments would be a lot less."

"Hold on a minute, why should I leave home? There's plenty of room in Mother's house."

Rex shrugged. "If that's what you want. I wasn't sure how Stella would take your turning up on the doorstep with a family in tow."

Come to think of it, he wasn't looking forward to turning up on Lanier's doorstep to tell him he could kiss his oldest daughter goodbye, because she and the kid were moving to Raleigh. Lanier needed her, but Rex needed her a hell of a lot more.

"Dammit, Rex, I know what you're trying to do, and it's not going to work! Okay, so Mother doesn't know about us yet. I can handle her. It's not the first time I've brought someone home with me. Mother wants me to be happy and Kim makes me happy."

"You're admitting she might be upset, though?"

"Yeah . . . well—maybe right at first. But once I explain everything and she understands how I feel, she'll come around. She always does."

"Taking a wife home with you is a bit different from inviting a buddy over for the weekend, Billy. What do you think Stella's going to say when you walk in with a woman on your arm?"

"Kim's not just a woman, she'll be my wife! Mother will have to accept her!" Billy's clean-cut good looks had the unfortunate effect of making him seem younger than his years. Dressed in white ducks and a yellow-striped Brookes Brothers shirt, he could easily have passed for a male model, right down to the petulant look on his face.

God, was I ever that young? Rex wondered. Leaning back, he gazed at the couple across the room from under lowered lids. "I expect you're right," he drawled lazily. A woman? She looked more like a kid who'd been denied a promised treat, quivering lip, big tearful blue eyes and all. At her best, Kim Lanier would never be half the woman her sister was, but that was Billy's problem, not his.

"Sounds like you've both thought things through pretty thoroughly. You're right. If this is what you want, I'm sure Stella will be happy for you."

He could feel Carrie inching forward on the velvet cushion. *Trust me, sugar. I haven't lost my mind yet.*

"Look, everything's cool, I keep telling you!" Billy insisted, and Rex allowed a sliver of stainless steel to show under his thick black lashes. "Just because Mother and Belinda think your Maddie's the greatest thing since sliced bread—"

"We're not talking about Maddie, we're talking about you and Kim. I just want to be sure you know exactly what you're getting into before it's too late to back out."

"Who's Maddie?" Kim asked.

"Nobody," Rex said.

"My big brother's—what is she, Rex? Your mistress? Your fiancée? Bel's been talking about—"

"What she is, is none of your business," Rex snapped. Sensing Carrie's unspoken questions, he figured it was time to get the discussion back on track. He'd tell her about Maddie later.

He was also going to have to tell Maddie about Carrie, and he wasn't particularly looking forward to either event. "Kim, what does your father think about your getting married?"

"He doesn't know." Kim's blue eyes focused on the soft, pale hands in her lap. She chewed her fingernails, Rex noted, and felt a sudden sympathy for her in spite of his impatience.

"Didn't you think you owed your family an explanation before you ran off and worried them half to death?" he asked in a mild tone.

"Why should I tell them anything? All Daddy does is grumble, and Carrie's too busy keeping Joanna out of trouble and chasing after her precious old cows to care about anything else!"

Hearing Carrie's soft gasp, Rex deliberately leaned back, slung one leg over the other and stretched his arm out across the back of the love seat. *Heads down, folks, she's about to blow!*

Her hands started talking before she ever opened her mouth, and Rex grinned. But if he'd expected her to counterattack, much less defend herself, he was in for a surprise. His arm brushed her shoulder, and she leaned forward, rejecting his support. He could almost feel the tension as she struggled to harness her flyaway temper.

"Kim, have you and Billy thought about how you're going to take care of a baby?"

"Oh—! You *would* think that! Not all of us are—"

"Kimberly Anne..."

"Well, it's none of your business. You've got no right to talk, anyway!"

Color drained from Carrie's face, making her eyes look enormous. Rex could cheerfully have throttled the brat. He covered Carrie's hands—unusually still for the moment—with his own. "I think your sister's trying to find out if there's any big hurry to your getting married, Kimberly." He looked at Billy. "Somehow I can't see Stella settling contentedly into grandmotherhood. Or were you thinking she could baby-sit while the two of you finish school?"

Billy jumped up and began pacing. To no one in particular, Rex observed, "Now, me, I kinda like kids. Always thought I'd like to have a few of my own when the time was right."

Like hell he had! One thing he'd always made clear from the start of any relationship was that he didn't want serious involvement, he wasn't interested in long-term commitment, and he had no intention of saddling himself with a family anytime in the near future.

On the other hand, a little girl who was half Carrie's...

Kim spoke up, and reluctantly, Rex had to admire her gumption. "Look, I'm not pregnant, if that's what you're thinking, Mr. Ryder." She looked defiantly at her sister. "Unlike some people I know, Billy and I don't plan on having children for a long time. He's still got three years of school left, and then he plans to study law. I'm going to get a job and help out."

"Then that pretty well settles matters, I'd say, wouldn't you, Carrie? With no kids on the way, Kim can support them both and pay Billy's tuition while—"

"Kim doesn't have to support me or pay my tuition, either. Mother does that."

"Okay, then. Stella will put you through school while Kim works to pay for the house. Or maybe just an apartment at first. Of course, you'd be losing equity in that case, but what the hell—a couple just starting out can't have everything. The important thing is you've got each other, right?''

"You can cut it out right now," Billy protested. "I know what you're trying to do, and it's not going to work! My wife doesn't have to get a job, I can take care of her!"

"You mean Stella can take care of the pair of you. Well . . . you know your mother better than I do."

Carrie leaned forward. "Kim, don't you know how hurt Daddy will be?''

"Why should he be hurt? He never pays any attention to anyone but Jo, and that's just because she has black hair, like Mama." Kim's eyes brimmed, but never quite overflowed. Her full bottom lip quivered pitifully, and Billy put his arm around her and glared at the other pair.

"Now look what you've done! She's crying!"

Carrie was evidently unmoved, either by Kim's tears or Billy's defense. "You know Daddy loves us both. He just—well, he's not good at showing it, but—"

"Daddy just doesn't want anyone to have any fun."

"That's not true. He's given you everything he possibly could—more than he could afford to give you, and you know it. If he's cross sometimes, it's only because he's so frustrated at having to get around on that cart of his."

"Well, anyway, it won't be that way with Billy and me. We've never had a single argument, have we, Billy?''

"How can you even consider marrying a man you've never argued with? What's going to happen when he comes home after a rotten day and snaps at you for not having supper ready?''

"Billy would never take his bad temper out on me. He loves me too much, don't you, sweetums?''

Sweetums turned every color of the rainbow and tugged at the neck of his open-throated shirt. "Kim's easy to get along with," he mumbled.

"As long as everything goes her way. Most people are easy to get along with under ideal circumstances, but circumstances aren't always ideal, even in the best of marriages."

"What do you know about it? Yours sure didn't last very long!" It was a taunt, and everyone recognized it as such, but Carrie didn't rise to the bait.

"That doesn't mean I don't know the difference between a good marriage and a bad one," Carrie said with more patience than Rex would have given her credit for. "One of the biggest dangers of marrying too young is that people change as they grow older. Sometimes they find out they're married to strangers. Look at Mama and Daddy."

"Or you and Don," Kim shot back, and Carrie nodded.

"Exactly," she said with a quiet dignity that made Rex want to take her in his arms and hold her until all the hurt was forgotten. "Regardless of how wonderful things might seem in the beginning, Kimmy, they don't always last. People go on growing, and sometimes they grow apart instead of together, until after a while there's nothing left to hold them together. They're like strangers."

"It won't be like that for Billy and me. You and Don had Joanna, and that didn't make any difference, so what are you trying to say?"

Carrie studied her clasped hands. "I don't know. Sometimes even children aren't enough when there's so much bitterness it gets in the way of whatever little love is left."

For a woman who never made it to college, Rex thought, Carrie Lanier had a good head on her shoulders. To think of all the time he'd wasted while he was growing up trying to figure out who he was and where he belonged in the cosmic scheme of things. Maybe he should have asked Carrie. She'd probably have screwed up her earnest little face and spouted off an answer that would have held him until he could figure out things for himself.

"Well, for your information, that's not going to happen to Billy and me. We've been in love for almost a whole year!"

Rex listened to them both, but he watched Carrie, his mind taking in her words, toying with them, and putting them into a slightly different context. He was nearly thirty-two. She was thirty. At Billy's age, he'd still been trying to mesh his idea of who he was with his father's. By now, he knew enough about himself to be pretty sure that what he'd wanted at seventeen, he still wanted.

And this time, he was old enough to go after it.

"Kim," Carrie was saying—Rex had missed part of her remarks. "I love you, and I only want you to be happy. You're right. Some couples do marry young, and it lasts forever. But more don't than do. If you want to take a chance on waking up one morning with a stranger in your bed, I guess I can't stop you. You'll probably make a couple of divorce lawyers happy, anyway."

You don't pull your punches, do you, lady? Rex stroked his jaw to hide a grin as he glanced over to see how his brother was taking all this.

Billy had dropped down onto a white wicker stool and was staring down at his hundred-and-sixty-dollar athletic shoes. He didn't look up.

Carrie sighed, and Rex's attention turned to her. Was she waiting for him to step in and administer the *coup de grace?* No, she wasn't quite done yet.

"Look, Kim, I know how you feel—"

"No, you don't! How could you know? You've never been in love, not even with Donald! You only married him because you had to!"

Oh, ho!

"That's beside the point. Kim, you've got your whole life ahead of you. You just barely turned eighteen."

"Which means I'm an adult!"

"Which means you can vote. You're not even old enough to drink in North Carolina, but that's beside the point, too."

"I'm old enough to get married, and you can't stop me!"

"No, I can't, but you're my sister, and I don't want you to—"

"You don't want me to have any fun! You're just like Daddy! Just because you and Daddy get your kicks from a bunch of smelly old cows, you think everybody else should, too!"

Rex looked from one to the other—from the pretty, petulant teenager to the woman who was struggling against an emotion he could only guess at. Carrie wanted to say something and didn't know how, her hands alternately curling and uncurling in her lap. He ached to help her out, to take away that look in her eyes.

"No, I can't stop you," she said finally. "And if this is what you're determined to do, then I'll stand up with you and do everything I can to smooth things over at home. But Kimmy, remember this. Love isn't all roses and dancing in the moonlight. It's sickness as well as health. It's worse as well as better. Will you still want Billy if worse comes to worse, or will you do like Mama did and run away? You know what happened to Daddy after she left. He got careless and he's paid for it ever since. Billy deserves better than that."

"You're just trying to make me change my mind," Kim argued, but she no longer sounded quite so sure.

"No, baby, I'm just trying to make sure you *know* your mind. If you do—if both of you are sure this is what you really want, then I won't say anything more, but if you have the slightest doubt..."

Kim peered sideways at Billy. He stopped cracking his knuckles long enough to shoot her a glance.

Carrie looked from one of them to the other, and Rex watched Carrie. Thought about what she'd said. Regardless of her brief marriage, he knew that here was a woman for all time. If he'd ever doubted it, he knew it now. Only how did she feel about it? About him? He knew he could make her want him—they were dynamite together.

Hell, she was dynamite all by herself!

But sex and marriage didn't always come in the same package, and before he could go any further, he had some unfinished business to take care of.

Five minutes later they were loitering in the parking lot, trying to figure out who would ride with whom. Billy wanted Kim to ride with him, and Rex wanted Carrie, but somehow, when they drove off, Kim was driving Billy's Mustang with Carrie as her passenger, and Billy was riding with Rex.

Long before they'd left Little Joe's World Famous Wedding Parlor, Rex was half tempted to wish the pair of them well, offer their services as best man and maid of honor, and then grab Carrie and head for the nearest license bureau.

But he didn't. Because Carrie was right. Those two weren't ready. Oh, they might've lucked out—it wasn't unheard of. But the statistics were pretty grim, and there wasn't enough maturity between the two of them to make him believe they could beat the odds.

"I'll call you tonight about picking up the car, Kim," Billy said.

"Don't forget to pick up your truck," Rex reminded Carrie.

She stood there under the blazing noonday sun, looking belligerent and sad and so damned beautiful, he wanted to sweep her up in his arms and keep her there for the next hundred years.

Carrie fumbled in her purse for her sunglasses. "I'll send you the money I owe you, Rex, and...thank you."

His smile never reached his eyes. He intended to collect a hell of a lot more than money, and if she didn't know it already, she soon would.

Rex drove, and he drove fast. Billy sat with his large hands hanging between his knees, staring straight ahead. When the silence became oppressive, he switched on the radio, but Rex could take only so much hard rock and Billy had a low tolerance for country and classical, so he switched it off again.

"You going to go on seeing her?" Rex asked.

"Yeah."

"What does Lanier think about it?"

Billy shrugged. "Who knows? I say hello, he grunts and goes back to his newspaper and that's the end of it."

"Carrie around much when you go there?"

"Nah. She's always got her nose stuck in a book—some kind of records, I guess. She's got a desk in one corner of the dining room, calls it her office. I see her kid sometimes. Nice girl. Tall. Dark. Must take after her old man. He was before my time."

Rex nodded absently, wondering if he'd made a mistake in letting her get away without some kind of an understanding.

Billy beat time on the dashboard with his fingertips. He took out his ostrich-skin wallet and counted his money. He sighed a few times, started to whistle and stopped, and then he said, "Kim's got this housekeeper who's got the weirdest eyes you've ever seen. One's blue and other one's kind of brownish green. Not bad-looking, though, for an old broad. Kim says she's got the hots for the old man. Can you beat it? And him in a wheelchair?"

Rex sent him a scathing look and they drove the next fifty-odd miles in silence.

After her initial panic over the bill, Carrie wrote a check for the towing and the repairs to her truck. She'd have to rush down to the bank first thing in the morning and deposit enough to cover it, and then call the dentist to see if she could postpone this month's payment for Jo's braces. Two weeks at summer camp in the mountains had just about wiped her out, without all this business.

"Sure you can make it home all right by yourself?" she asked Kim as she climbed up into the familiar rump-sprung seat.

"Car-rie!" Kim clashed the gears and Carrie decided that Billy was either a fool or head over heels in love to have lent her his precious red Mustang.

Her mind turned back to Rex. He hadn't said anything about calling her or seeing her again. But then, why should he? Mission accomplished, and all that. And if they happened to have gotten in a little too deep for a few hours, that wasn't exactly a commitment.

On his part, at least.

Carrie sighed. She'd done more of that in the past few days than she'd done in all her previous thirty years. She wasn't a sigher by nature, any more than she was a crier, but she had a feeling she was going to be doing a lot more of both before she got her head together again.

* * *

Rex dressed with greater care than usual that night. By the time he'd dropped Billy off, stopped by to close up the cabin and driven on to Raleigh, he was wiped out, but he'd called Maddie, half hoping she'd gone on to the beach without him. She was home and not at all surprised to hear from him, in spite of the fact that he'd told her he was going to be spending a couple of weeks at his cabin. Alone.

Now, dammit, she'd be thinking he couldn't stay away from her. He had never encouraged her to feel that way, but to be fair, he had never exactly discouraged her, either. Maddie was a nice woman. Intelligent, attractive, sexually experienced, and a comfortable companion when he felt like companionship.

The only trouble was, after seeing Carrie again, he knew he could never settle for anything less.

Ten

"There's simply *got* to be a diplomatic way to say no!" Maddie said as she flung aside the bridal magazine she'd been glancing through when Rex arrived. Rex had taken one look at the thing and blanched. "Damn, would you believe pea-green chiffon? With puff sleeves and flounces, yet? I swear I'll shoot the first person who laughs."

It didn't sound particularly bridal. He began to relax. "This would be a . . . uh? . . ."

"A bridesmaid's gown, what else?"

"The bride's a close friend of yours?"

She spared him a scathing look. "Not after this. You wouldn't believe how much I've spent in the last few years on bridesmaid's outfits, and not one of them is fit to be worn for anything else." Leading the way into the living room, she plopped down onto the sofa, shoving several more magazines with a distinctly bridal flavor onto the floor.

Rex sent them a wary look. He jutted his chin and loosened his tie. "Well!" he stated conclusively, after which the conversation languished. "Have you had dinner?" he asked desperately.

"I snacked earlier. Have you?"

He hadn't, but said he had, and she offered him a drink.

Rex poured a drink that was largely water and sat it down untasted. He'd always felt comfortable before in the cream-and-beige room with its fruitwood accents. Maddie had impeccable, if rather unexciting, taste. Suddenly, it struck him as too drab. Too safe.

"You're a problem solver." *He was?* "What's your solution for a woman who's always a bridesmaid and never a bride?"

A bead of sweat trickled down the hollow of his back. "You could always decline the honor."

"Better yet, I could get even by getting married, making every last one of them take part, and picking out tacky little gowns that are impossible for anyone over sixteen. Think they'd get the message?"

Rex managed a strangled sound that passed for a reply. If that was supposed to be his cue, he chose to ignore it. The sooner he got this thing over and done with, the better. He didn't like hurting people, especially people he liked.

Reaching for his drink, he carried it across to the window and stared out. *Just tell her the truth, man! She can handle it.*

Yeah? Are you so sure?

He thought of his wild acres on the river. He thought of Carrie in her faded jeans, her wrinkled denim shirt and her scuffed boots, with her hair blowing wild around her head. "Maddie, about us...I've been thinking. It seems to me that you and I are—"

She didn't wait for him to finish. "I've been thinking, too, Rex. I'll be thirty-five on my next birthday."

God, here it comes. He should have told her right off the bat. Now she was going to hint, and he'd have to hedge, and they'd both be embarrassed, and he wouldn't do that to her for the world.

"Maddie—"

"It's got nothing to do with my so-called biological clock, you understand. The thing is—"

"Look, before you go any further, I'd better tell you why I came over tonight."

"Don't. Please." Her tone was soft, her blue eyes slightly evasive. "Just let me say this and get it over, will you? We've always been honest with each other. That's one of the things I've always prized about our relationship. You're a wonderful man, Rex. What we've had has been very precious to me."

I don't want to hear this. Don't make it any tougher on me, Maddie, because I don't want to hurt you any more than I have to.

Sighing, he dropped onto a beige fruitwood chair, resigned to hearing her out. He owed her that much, but she was only making it more painful for them both by dragging things out into the open this way. "Thank you, Maddie," he said quietly. "I've always valued our, uh—friendship, too."

"It's just that you stay so busy so much of the time. I can't plan my social life because I never know when you'll be taking off for parts unknown." He didn't miss the pleading note in her voice.

She was going to cry. He was going to tell her it was all over between them because he was in love with another woman, and things were going to get messy. Dammit, they'd both gone into this affair with their eyes wide open, and now she was changing the rules on him. Was that fair? If he'd known she was going to get serious, he would have bowed out a long time ago.

Maddie's well-modulated voice interrupted his thoughts. "—And anyway, what difference does it make where you are if you're not here when I need an escort? Drew's always been willing to fill in for you at the last minute—Andrew Bricker, by the way—he's with Adams-Price over at the Research Triangle."

"What is this, some kind of confession?"

"No, it's not a confession! I'm trying to explain, that's all, because I owe you that much, at least."

Rex felt the first cool hint of relief. He waited, not daring to anticipate. But if she was trying to tell him what he thought—what he *hoped*—she was trying to tell him, then he could be out of here in fifteen minutes, and on Carrie's doorstep in another forty-five.

"It's not as if what we had was headed anywhere in particular. You do understand, don't you, Rex? It was always open-ended, on both our parts. I thought that was understood."

Inhaling deeply, Rex blew his breath out in a single gust, and tried not to let his relief show. Relief, hell. Try glee! Try so damned happy to get out of this thing with no bloodshed on either side that he felt like turning cartwheels across her beige Berber carpet!

"Yeah, sure, honey. This guy Bricker—are you in love with him?"

"I'm...attracted to him. I like him. We're unusually compatible."

"You're talking marriage, huh?"

"What if I am? Andrew's forty-five. Statistics prove that married men live longer than single ones. I'm assuming that works for women, too."

"It's a crazy reason to get married, but if it makes you happy, you have my blessings."

As if recognizing the need to bring things to a neat conclusion, Maddie stood and strolled over to straighten a bland blue-and-beige landscape. Rex stood, too. His gaze wandered over her back from the crown of her smooth blond pageboy to the inch-and-a-half heels of her tan pumps. She was everything a man could want in a woman. Sexy in an understated way, with flawless features and excellent taste in clothes. She had sense of humor—at least she had the sense to laugh at his jokes once she recognized them as jokes—and she probably earned about twice what he did in an average year.

The trouble was, she wasn't Carrie.

"You ought to try it before it's too late, Rex." She smiled at him. Her teeth were an orthodontist's dream. "Statistically speaking, it would be a smart move for any single man."

"Yeah, well... could be you're right," he replied, striving to sound casual and missing it by a country mile. "Maybe I'll get lucky and meet a woman who knocks me so far off base I can't do anything *but* marry her. They say it happens that way sometimes."

"I wouldn't hold my breath," Maddie said dryly. "Raging hormones aside, maybe it's time you looked around for a compatible woman who'll be there for you when you need her and won't be driven out of her mind by boredom when you don't. My suggestion is an older woman, one of those dedicated homemaker types who'll be content to can peaches and crochet rugs while you run around playing cops and robbers with your little computer."

He took the not-too-subtle put-down in stride. Maddie was inclined to judge a man by the salary he commanded. Rex had never bothered to try to explain that no honest man went to work for the state government in hopes of getting rich. Not unless he suffered from a severe deficiency of integrity.

"Maybe you're right."

"I know I'm right. Give it a chance, Rex. You might like it."

"I'll consider it, then," he promised her gravely. "For the sake of my health."

To his credit, Rex managed to contain his broad grin until he got outside. It was done. He was free. And Carrie was waiting.

Both the grin and the euphoria faded when he saw that his right front tire was flat. He uttered a succinct four-letter word and then took a minute to rein in his impatience before getting out his jack. He was on the homestretch now. All he had to do now was tackle Ralph Lanier, and then set about winning the kid over to his side.

A daughter... Yeah, he could kind of get into that. Carrie's baby. She'd be something, if she had half her mama's spunk.

Carrie stared at the page of neat entries in her record book and willed the phone to ring. She looked at the clock and then back at the phone. He hadn't said he'd call her, but she had hoped.

Maybe tomorrow...

She stared at the last entry. Weight, measurements, breeding date, sire.

Sire. She could picture a miniature Rex in tiny denim overalls, with impudent gray eyes and a shaggy crop of near-black hair. Ralph Rexford Ryder? Would that be too much to visit on a small boy? How would Jo like a baby brother?

She glanced at the phone again and sighed. If he'd planned to see her again, he would have said something, wouldn't he? Billy had promised to call Kim and he'd already called twice, just as if they hadn't parted less than twenty-four hours ago.

The phone rang, and Carrie nearly jumped out of her skin. Before she could snatch it up, the ringing stopped. Kim yelled down from her bedroom. "I've got it!"

Carrie's shoulders slumped, and she forced herself to concentrate on the ledger. She was up to her ears in bloodlines and weight gains when Kim wandered into the dining room a few minutes later. "Billy's coming over." She eased herself onto the edge of the scarred desk, her hair wrapped in a towel and her face masked in something pink and shiny. "Do you think Daddy'll be mad?"

"Why should he be? He ought to be used to it by now."

"I wish he and Lib would come out of the closet and be done with it. Maybe it would sweeten him up some."

"What closet?" Carrie murmured, only half paying attention.

"The bedroom closet, silly. All this sneaking around can't be healthy."

"Kimberly! That's *Daddy* you're talking about!"

"So? He's a man, isn't he? Don't let that wheelchair fool you, I've seen the way he and Lib act when they think nobody sees them."

Carrie flopped back in the ancient, oak swivel chair and stared at her baby sister. "I think you've got sex on the brain. Honestly, Kim, just because—"

"Just because nothing. You're never around the house long enough to see what's been going on right under our noses. You're always out mucking around in the barns or chasing some stupid cow around a pasture."

"And if I didn't, who do you think would?"

"Daddy? Ody? Jo?"

"Daddy can't do everything, and neither can Ody, and Jo still has to finish school. And before you tell me again that we ought to hire another manager, we can't afford it."

"I still wish he'd marry her, and then we wouldn't ever have to worry about her quitting. Daddy would *really* be impossible to live with if Lib took off."

"Why should she? She gets a decent salary, plus room and board and all the same benefits the other farm workers get. If you're dreaming up all this stuff to take my mind off that wild-goose chase you sent me on, you can forget it, because I don't believe it."

"I don't have to dream up anything." Kim began peeling off strips of pink from her cheeks, dropping them on a stack of feed bills. "Only four of us sleep upstairs." Kim and Jo shared the largest room, Lib had the one at the back of the house, and Carrie the front. Ralph's room was on the first floor. "The stairs creak, and I know it's not Jo or me."

"It's an old house. Maybe it's termites."

"Yeah, and maybe Lib likes to raid the refrigerator, but my bet is there's some good old-fashioned hanky-panky going on right under this roof."

"Daddy and *Lib Swanson?*" Good Lord, was there an epidemic around here? It must be something in the water.

The heat under the metal shed roof was overpowering. Carrie, leaning over the fence to prod a recalcitrant yearling through the chute, wiped a filthy sleeve across her eyes in an effort to remove the top layer of sweat and dirt. She would have brought in the big electric fan if she hadn't been afraid it would spook the cattle. Besides, the dust was bad enough, as it was.

It was a typical June. The earliest blackberries were at their best, the flies at their worst; it was invariably dry when they needed rain and invariably wet when they didn't.

It also happened to be the busiest month of all on a cattle farm. "Ody, did you get these scales checked last week?"

The grizzled old man who had worked for Ralph Lanier's father, and who, except for the fact that he couldn't read and was too stubborn to admit it, would have taken over the entire operation after Ralph Lanier had had his accident, allowed as how he'd had the dagblamed things checked the way he always did, and she hadn't ought to nag at him about it. "Women," he muttered.

Carrie knew Odyous had never liked working for a woman, but she didn't know what she could do about it. It hadn't been her choice, either, but somehow, she'd been stuck with the job. She had to make a living for Jo and herself, and someone had to dose the cows, chase calves, breed the heifers and fill out all those endless forms.

With the last few heads now moving through the chute, Carrie stepped down from the fence, wiped her eyes again and resettled her broad-brimmed straw hat. Was that a cloud of dust coming up the main drive?

"Ody, wasn't Buck coming over today to look at that baler?"

"Nope. Done that yestiddy."

One of Kim's friends, then. With school just out, they were enjoying the holiday before looking for jobs. Lord knows, if Kim had shown half an inclination to make herself useful, Carrie would have snapped her up in a minute. Just keeping up with the office work would've been a big help, and she wouldn't even have had to get dirty. Kim had always had a low tolerance for the grubby end of the beef business. Thank goodness Jo seemed to love it.

"Whoo, hey, get on in here!" Carrie leaped back up on the third rail, waving her hat at a yearling who insisted on head-butting every animal in sight. "Precocious little devil, aren't you? Next you'll be trying to mount my little girls. Wait until you grow up, stud.''

"That there'un's gonna win us a ribbon or two. He'll top old K.D.'s weight before he's eighteen month old, less'n I miss my guess.''

"Better put him in the south pasture. I don't want him tangling with one of the bigger boys.'' Bending at the hips, Carrie draped her arms over the top rail and admired the young bull she was bringing along as a replacement for old King's Dominion. She used a breeder service on the two largest herds, but for sentimental reasons more than anything else, she kept one small herd of purebred Black Angus. They didn't gain as fast, and they weren't quite as hardy, but they were so beautiful. In her grandfather's day, the farm had produced a purebred product that invariably graded out high-choice to prime, depending on finish, but times had changed. Nobody wanted fat beef any longer. She had finally convinced her father to crossbreed for sport vigor, and then triple-cross for leaner beef and faster growth.

Rex parked under the shade of a giant red oak, some fifty yards away from the shed. His footsteps muffled by the dry red clay, he could hear her yipping, see her reach over the fence to swat a balky calf on the rump with her hat. He halted just short of the metal utility building as time eclipsed. He reminded himself that he was no longer seventeen, even though his body reacted with the same old enthusiasm. Either he was going to have to learn to control his urges, or he was going to have to work on his stamina. He could see them now, white-haired, bones brittle with age, sending the grandbabies off to the movies so they could dive into the sack together. If aerobics was considered healthy, sex had to be even better. It was a hell of a lot more fun, at least.

Ah, Carrie, Carrie. Rex paused some twenty feet away and watched. Hot, dusty and sweaty, she was still more beautiful to him than any other woman could ever be. He only wished her daughter had had red hair, too.

A leathery gray-haired man in work denim came stumping around the side of the shed just as Carrie swung around on the fence, hanging there by her elbows and boot heels. She looked stunned to see him.

"Carrie? Honey, I—"

"Don't I know you, boy?' asked the old man suspiciously.

"Ody, why don't you go call Buck and see if he's going to get out here today?"

"I told ye, he done come yestiddy."

"Ody, just go, will you? I want to talk to Rex. Alone, please."

"I ain't goin' off and leavin' you alone, missy. I'll be right there in the shed, y'hear?"

Carrie smiled, and Rex felt his heart melt and run right down into his loafers. No way did it make sense, this thing he felt for her, but he was long past trying to figure it out.

"That's fine, Ody. This is Rex Ryder, who helped me chase Kim down to South Carolina. Rex, Odyous Smith, Daddy's right-hand man. He practically runs this place single-handed."

Rex had a pretty good idea of who ran it, but if she wanted to play it that way, who was he to argue? He extended a hand to the old man and after a noticeable hesitation, it was gripped by a horny paw and quickly released. He waited while Odyous Smith examined him from the toes of his dusty shoes to the crown of his freshly trimmed hair, missing nothing in between.

After the old man had stomped off, grumbling about no-good young troublemakers and fool-headed women, Rex

turned his full attention back to Carrie, who was still clinging to the fence. "You planning on staying up there all
day?"

"If I'd known you were coming—"

"You knew."

As if in a daze, she shook her head. "You didn't say so."

He moved in closer, corralling her with a pair of hard,
tanned arms. "You knew," he repeated, gazing deeply into
her bittersweet-chocolate eyes. Eyes which were, for once,
on a level with his. "We have some unfinished business,
lady."

Carrie was beginning to display definite signs of ner-
vousness. "Look, why don't you—ah, go somewhere and
do something and let me run home and wash my face and
hands?"

And soak in a tub of scented water, she added silently.
*And slather on quarts of scented body lotion. And put on
something soft and feminine and try, for once in my life, not
to look and smell like I've been rolling in the feed lot.*

"Carrie, I've finished the first part of my unfinished
business. I don't want to waste any more time getting down
to the most important part."

"Oh. Well, if we have to talk now, let's go over under the
oak tree. If there's a breeze anywhere, it'll be there." She
tried and failed to duck under his arms.

"I didn't kiss you goodbye when we left Little Joe's place.
That means you owe me two."

"I don't owe you anything. At least not kisses. Rex, let
me down from here, will you? You're clean, and I'm filthy."

"That's no excuse."

"Dammit, Rex, this isn't fair!"

"Who's talking fair? I'm talking winning, and if that
takes down-and-dirty, I'm more than ready."

Carrie's lips twitched, and she tried to overcome it with a frown. "Well, if it's down-and-dirty you want, you've already lost the match."

"Yeah? We'll see about that."

He leaned closer, and there wasn't one blessed thing she could do about it. Just before she closed her eyes, Carrie released the fence and tumbled forward into his arms. "Damn you, you always catch me at a disadvantage!" she muttered, and then he kissed her.

A long time later, Rex lifted his face. His heart was thundering under his once-crisp white shirt, and his hands were none too steady. "Lady, if you're at a disadvantage now, I hope to hell you never get the upper hand."

Carrie looked equally dazed. Her lips were soft and gleaming from his kisses. Rex couldn't stop staring. It occurred to him that her lips were probably the cleanest part of her face.

It also occurred to him that he didn't care if she'd been splashing in a hog wallow, she was what he wanted—*all* he wanted—and this time he was damned well going to have her!

"We've got some talking to do," he said hoarsely.

"You already said that."

"Bear with me. It's worth repeating."

"Rex, I absolutely—"

He closed off her words with another kiss—this one gentle and searching instead of throbbing with passion as the first one had been.

"You were saying?"

She gulped in a breath of air and tried again. "Rex, I absolutely refuse to—" Gesturing wildly, she nearly lost her balance.

He kissed her once more, and to Carrie's everlasting shame, she clung to him. She could no more turn away from his kisses than she could sprout wings and fly.

Even so, she managed a stern look when he lifted his head. "Would you please stop doing that?"

"Nope."

"I can't think when you're kissing me," she wailed.

"Good." He grinned, his eyelids at half-mast, and with one hand gripping the fence and the other clutching Rex's shoulder, Carrie jutted her chin and tried to exert some authority.

"Are you going to let me go or not?"

"Nope." He pinned her against the fence, one hand on either side. It was a novel and thoroughly enjoyable situation.

"Rex, don't make me hurt you," she threatened.

Swallowing the urge to laugh, Rex considered her five-foot-two, ninety-nine pounds, and compared it to his own six-one, hundred-seventy-eight. "No, ma'am," he said, laughter simmering just under the surface of his deep drawl. "We wouldn't want that to happen."

She released the fence and jabbed a finger under his nose, but before she could utter a sound, he went on. "Carrie, have dinner with me tonight?"

"Dinner?"

"Yeah, you know... turnip greens and hot pepper vinegar, corn bread—all your favorite foods?"

She shot him a suspicious look. "Knowing you, you'd probably take me to the nearest steak house."

Rex tried to look suitably aghast, falling lamentably short of his goal. But a few minutes later, he was grinning from ear to ear as he strode back to his car. "No way, sweetheart," he murmured. "Next time we meet, it's going to be on my turf!"

* * *

Carrie refused to allow Rex to pick her up. She'd agreed to meet him at his cabin, but she wanted the independence her own transportation afforded her. If she'd learned one lesson this past weekend it was that things tended to get out of hand when she was all but a prisoner to a man she couldn't resist if her life depended on it.

It was dusk when she pulled up in front of the rustic, three-room cabin. She was running late because of a call from Jo, who wanted permission to go home from camp with her new best friend from Asheville. Not knowing the girl or her parents, Carrie had had to deny permission, and explain why, all on a collect call.

Rex's car, topped by a layer of dust, was parked off to one side, and there were lights glowing from every window. The place was so wild and off the beaten track, she hadn't been certain he even had electricity, but obviously he did.

"Welcome," he said quietly from the open door.

He'd only welcomed her, Carrie told herself. "Why do I feel like a fly being invited into the spider's parlor? Here." She thrust a foil-wrapped package at him. "Lib's coconut cake."

Pink, Rex decided, was her color. He particularly liked the big pearl buttons down the front.

He gave her time to look around, and tried to see the place through her eyes.

"Nice," she observed, and he nodded. It *was* nice, the inside walls varnished, with the chinking showing white between the logs. The furniture was large, plain and sturdy, running to oak and black leather. The large open area encompassed living room, kitchen and dining room, and there were three doors opening off the walls.

"Bedroom, junk room and bath. Want the grand tour first, or shall we eat?" He indicated the table, beautifully set with handmade pottery dishes, stoneware wineglasses, and wood-handled flatware.

"I'll tour later, if it's all the same to you. I'm starved!" But even as she spoke, Carrie knew she wouldn't be able to force down a bite. Had he suddenly grown taller? Surely his shoulders hadn't been that wide this morning? And she knew good and well his eyes were darker now. Normally a silvery gray, they looked dark as pitch!

"Um...this is pretty," she blurted. "Billy said you built it by yourself. I didn't know—that is, you must've..." Having lost the thread of whatever she'd been trying to say, she fell silent.

Rex seated her at the round table and set out a platter of sliced ham and several assorted side dishes. "Stella's cook took pity on me. Between Amy and your Lib, I reckon we won't starve tonight."

The words were about food, but his eyes were saying something altogether different. Carrie accepted every dish he handed her and dutifully filled her plate. Either her heart was going to pop right out of her blouse, or she was going to be sick to her stomach. She hadn't been this nervous since the time she'd shown her first bottle-raised bull at the State Fair.

"Wine?" Without waiting for an answer, Rex poured her a glassful. Carrie gulped down half of it and then studiously cut an entire slice of ham into tiny bites. How many times had she corrected Jo for doing the same thing?

Would Rex be furious? Would he like her? Oh, Lord, she was going to be sick.

Drawing a deep breath, she expelled it and then gazed up helplessly into Rex's amused eyes. "I don't think I'm very hungry," she said huskily. "Rex, we need to talk."

Rex gave up even pretending to eat. With his whole future at stake, food was the last thing on his mind. "Where do you want me to start, at the beginning or the middle?"

Where did she want *him* to start? Carrie, being no fool, grasped at the reprieve. "Maybe you'd better start at the end."

Her smile was distinctly wobbly, but Rex figured it was an improvement over the way she'd looked when she'd first stepped inside his house. Antoinette climbing up onto the platform couldn't have looked more wary.

"Okay, do you want the whole bit—white satin, a flock of bridesmaids and a six-story cake, or do you want to bypass the trimmings and get on to the main event?"

Carrie's eyes widened. Her fork clattered to the floor, but neither of them paid the least bit of attention.

"Carrie? Honey? Did you hear what I said? I know some women want the whole shooting match, with picture albums to prove it. I can get Belinda started organizing it if you want. God knows, she could organize an ice-skating party for the devil himself. On the other hand, there's a lot to be said for efficiency."

"Efficiency?" She croaked.

"I know a place down in—"

"Rex, maybe you'd better try starting at the beginning, after all."

"Oh. Okay, here goes. Better late than never, to coin a cliché."

Carrie wailed. "Re-ex!" and he left his seat and came around, lifting her out of her chair.

"Sorry, honey. I'm kinda new at this business of proposing. I've never done it before."

"Proposing?" she whispered.

His arms went around her, and then somehow they were both sprawled across the king-size sofa. A book of advanced crossword puzzles and one on the criminal justice system toppled to the floor, and Rex managed to catch a pitcher of full-blown roses just before it crashed down, too.

It took time, but both Rex and Carrie knew it was the only way for them. There was too much history, too many misunderstanding. Rex held her on his lap while he told her of his own feelings about those few brief, magical weeks before he'd left town. About the restlessness that had followed him through the years. About all the times he had wondered about her. About the letter he had written, that she had never received. About Maddie.

"I even thought about showing up on your doorstep and becoming a sort of honorary uncle to your kid."

"Why didn't you?" Carrie whispered. By now her blouse had unbuttoned itself, and Rex was sliding a hand under her back to find the catch to her bra. *Now,* she thought frantically. *Tell him now!*

"I was afraid I'd end up taking out your husband, which wouldn't have furthered my cause very much."

She didn't dare ask. She hardly dared breathe! "What cause?"

His arms tightened around her, and she closed her eyes, praying that if this were a dream, she would sleep forever. "Don't you know by now, Carrie? I always meant to come back and marry you. I thought we understood each other."

"I thought so, too," she whispered, melting as his hand moved over her breast. "Only, you went away...."

"But I came back, remember? And you were already married."

Carrie closed her eyes briefly, then stared at her clasped hands. "I didn't have much choice, Rex. At least, none that I could live with. When I found out I was pregnant, I knew how Daddy would feel. Don had been after me to go out with him. He . . . he claimed to love me, but I think it was mostly because I wasn't interested in him.''

She swallowed hard and darted another look at Rex, to find the color blanched from his face, his eyes and hair standing out in sharp contrast to his pallor. ''So I—'' she stumbled, took a deep breath, and blurted out the rest ''— I asked him if he would be interested in marrying me, even if I was pregnant with another man's baby. I never pretended to love him, but . . .'' Here she faltered. To this day, she felt guilty for marrying a decent man and turning him into a cruel and bitter one. She accepted the blame, had told no one, nor would she ever. It had been a bad bargain, and it hadn't lasted. Thank God.

''Are you saying—'' Rex began, his voice as raspy as an old saw. ''You were pregnant when I left? God, Carrie, why didn't you tell me? Why the hell did you let me go off, not knowing? Did you think I wouldn't *care?* That I wouldn't want our baby?'' He lowered his face in his hands, and Carrie waited, afraid to move, afraid to speak.

Finally, he lifted his head and stared at her. His eyes were dry, but tormented. ''Why?'' he repeated softly.

''Because I didn't know until after you'd gone. I couldn't go to Daddy—I certainly couldn't go to your parents.''

''So you turned to a stranger,'' he said bitterly.

Slowly, she nodded. ''I did what I thought was best for Joanna.''

''Joanna,'' Rex murmured. His color was returning, and he no longer looked as if he might strike out at something.

''John Rex Ryder. It was the closest I could come without being too obvious. I considered Rexanna, but—''

Rex's sharp burst of laughter was like broken glass. ''Thank God for small favors. Joanna. Joanna . . . Jennings?''

"Lanier. I took back our name for both of us."

"Joanna Ryder. Jo Ryder. Jo and Carrie Ryder."

"You'll never know how many times I thought about sending you a picture of her, Rex. You would've known right off. She looks so much like you."

"Why didn't you?"

"I didn't know where you were," she said simply, and he lifted her two hands and brought them up to his face, closing his eyes for a moment.

Carrie waited. She had waited so long. "I told myself I was a fool for wasting my life, that you were probably married to some tall, gorgeous woman with long fingernails who plays tennis and calls every man she meets dah-ling."

Chuckling, Rex leaned over and buried a kiss in her throat, and Carrie felt as if she'd been through another tornado and come out miraculously unscathed.

"Why should I settle for a tall, gorgeous tennis player when I could have a short, hot-tempered tractor jockey?"

"You really know how to make a woman feel wanted, don't you?"

"I do my modest best," he said. Rising, he scooped her up and headed for the bedroom, a broad grin creasing his lean cheeks. "Here I'm doing my best to propose to the mother of my child, and all she can do is complain. Sometimes I wonder why I bother."

"I do, too. Can I tell you something, Rex?"

"Anything but goodbye, sweetheart," he said, lowering her tenderly to the brown linen spread.

"I love you." She heaved a gusty sigh. "There! You have no idea how good it feels just to be able to say the words out loud."

Rex's eyes went from pewter to pitch-black as the pupils all but eclipsed the irises. "I love you, too, Carrie Lanier. I always have, only I've never been good at loving. Didn't believe in myself enough, I guess. But I've always believed in you. And when I think of all the time we've wasted—"

"We don't have to waste any more, do we?"

He went to work on her pink button-front skirt and then yanked his own shirt off over his head. "Are you saying what I think you're saying?"

"That I'd rather skip the rice and the rigmarole and head for the border?"

"That, too, but first…" Rex murmured as he shed the last of his clothes and came down beside her. She was wearing white cotton underwear. "I can't decide which I prefer as a trousseau," he told her. "Orchid lace with navy sneakers and a brown leather belt, or white cotton."

"Are you going to talk all night?" she whispered, love and sheer devilment gleaming in her dark eyes. "I have to be home by five in the morning to get started on the last two fields of wheat before the weather breaks."

"Are all you cowgirls so practical? Remind me sometime between now and daybreak to talk to you about finding us a place halfway between my work and yours, and about driving up to this camp and meeting my daughter and asking her permission to marry her mother. In the meantime…"

In the meantime was sheerest bliss. "Carrie, Carrie, what kind of spell did you put on me? Whatever it is—" he stroked her eyelids with the tip of his tongue "—I hope it lasts forever, because you've ruined me for any other woman."

His touch was light and tantalizing. Breathing erratically, Carrie began to move restlessly. "Rex, what are you trying to do, drive me wild?"

"Trying to—" He began to string a trail of nibbling kisses down the side of her throat, over one sensitive breast, and on to the other. "To make up for lost time."

Carrie shuddered and clutched at his shoulders to keep herself anchored in space. There was no such thing as lost time, she thought distractedly. Time began now.

By the time Rex knelt over her and gazed down at her flushed face, her eyes were molten with need. Proudly, aggressively male, he addressed himself to that unexpressed need. His hands on her thighs, he lowered his head and kissed the vulnerable area of her navel. He buried a dozen small kisses in the crease of each thigh, and then brushed a dozen more on her soft, fiery mound.

And then, in one swift stroke, he entered her. She groaned. Rex shuddered and closed his eyes. He stroked her slowly, trying desperately to make it last, to make it perfect for her, but there was no holding back. "You're so small—so tight—I don't want to hurt you, precious," he whispered. Every rock-hard muscle and sinew in his body was trembling as he fought for control.

Her eyes clung to his, urging him on. "I won't break," she promised, her hands flying like butterflies, touching him here, there—and there, too. "Please, Rex!"

"Wait, love, be still, or it'll be over before it begins."

But Carrie had already waited a lifetime, and that was long enough.

Rex awoke first. It took several minutes to convince himself that this was Carrie—and that she was truly his own. He had a family. He belonged to someone—two someones who belonged to him!

"Sweetheart," he whispered, stirring tendrils of coppery hair against her cheek.

Carrie swatted at whatever had tickled her, and murmured sleepily, "Whazzamatter?"

"Did you ever give me an answer?"

She blinked and rolled over to find herself imprisoned against a hard, hairy chest. Yawning, she began to explore with her toes. A foot. A big one. A calf—also hairy. The bony thing had to be a knee. Feeling deliciously languid, she lifted her own knee and swiveled into a cozier alignment.

"Watch it, short stuff, that's dangerous territory."

"Promise?" She grinned and nuzzled his throat, savoring the salty, sexy taste of his skin. "What answer?"

"White lace? Garden parties? Country club receptions?"

"I've never set foot in a country club in my life," she retorted indignantly.

"Hey, I'm not accusing you of anything." Chuckling, he rolled over on top of her, and said, "You may as well know that if Belinda gets wind of this affair, we're going to be tied up in red tape and satin ribbon for the next six months."

"Six months! But Jo's camp's over this Friday. I thought— That is, unless you'd like to let your sister—"

"No way. Saturday sounds good to me, if Jo agrees."

"She'll love it. I can't imagine what Kim's going to say, but Jo will be on our side, I'm certain of it."

"Good," Rex said with open satisfaction. "Because it just so happens that I know a place..."

Carrie took up the refrain. "Just over the border—"

"Where marryin's quick—"

"And made to order!"

Rex closed his eyes in blissful contemplation as he gathered her warm, sweet nakedness against him. "I wish it could be today," he murmured.

"So do I, but we still need to discuss what we're going to do about my work and yours, and where we're going to live and things like that."

"Mmm. Later," Rex promised.

And much, much later, they got finally around to it.

*   *   *   *   *

SILHOUETTE® Desire™

COMING NEXT MONTH

#721 SHIPWRECKED!—Jackie Merritt
Miles Leighton was insufferable, rude, and Lexie Wallis couldn't *stand* him! Then they were stranded on a desert isle, and a bump on the head turned Miles from dreadful to dream boat....

#722 FLIRTING WITH TROUBLE—Cathie Linz
Determined to expose a gambling ring, librarian Nicole Larson was prepared to risk it all. And after one look at sexy undercover detective Chase Ellis, she knew she was flirting with trouble.

#723 PRINCESS McGEE—Maura Seger
Lucas Messina wanted revenge on Lorelei McGee for his uncle's death. Yet when he found she wasn't the ice princess he expected, how could he do anything but fall in love?

#724 AN UNSUITABLE MAN FOR THE JOB—Elizabeth Bevarly
Alexis Marchand thought Ramsey Walker was an arrogant, overgrown adolescent. He thought *she* was a prude. Could a tug-of-war between these two opposites lead to a perfect match?

#725 SOPHIE'S ATTIC—Robin Elliott
Hot on the trail of his ex-partner's murderer, secret agent Tyson McDonald knew he had to protect his friend's daughter, sultry Sophie Clarkson. But who would protect her from *him?*

#726 MIDNIGHT RIDER—Cait London
July's *Man of the Month*, Dan Blaylock, had to keep his hands off Hannah Jordan years ago. But now, the smart-mouthed, stubborn woman needed a rough rider to keep an eye on her....

AVAILABLE NOW—June Grooms:

#715 THE CASE OF THE CONFIRMED BACHELOR
Diana Palmer

#716 MARRIED TO THE ENEMY
Ann Major

#717 ALMOST A BRIDE
Raye Morgan

#718 NOT *HIS* WEDDING!
Suzanne Simms

#719 McCONNELL'S BRIDE
Naomi Horton

#720 BEST MAN FOR THE JOB
Dixie Browning

FREE GIFT OFFER

To receive your free gift, send us the specified number of proofs-of-purchase from any specially marked Free Gift Offer Harlequin or Silhouette book with the Free Gift Certificate properly completed, plus a check or money order (do not send cash) to cover postage and handling payable to Harlequin/Silhouette Free Gift Promotion Offer. We will send you the specified gift.

FREE GIFT CERTIFICATE

ITEM	A. GOLD TONE EARRINGS	B. GOLD TONE BRACELET	C. GOLD TONE NECKLACE
# of proofs-of-purchase required	3	6	9
Postage and Handling	$2.25	$2.75	$3.25
Check one	☐	☐	☐

Name: _____

Address: _____

City: _____ Province: _____ Postal Code: _____

Mail this certificate, specified number of proofs-of-purchase and a check or money order for postage and handling to: HARLEQUIN/SILHOUETTE FREE GIFT OFFER 1992, P.O. Box 622, Fort Erie, Ontario L2A 5X3. Requests must be received by July 31, 1992.

PLUS—Every time you submit a completed certificate with the correct number of proofs-of-purchase, you are automatically entered in our MILLION DOLLAR SWEEPSTAKES! No purchase or obligation necessary to enter. See below for alternate means of entry and how to obtain complete sweepstakes rules.

MILLION DOLLAR SWEEPSTAKES
NO PURCHASE OR OBLIGATION NECESSARY TO ENTER

To enter, hand-print (mechanical reproductions are not acceptable) your name and address on a 3" ×5" card and mail to Million Dollar Sweepstakes 6097, c/o either P.O. Box 9056, Buffalo, NY 14269-9056 or P.O. Box 621, Fort Erie, Ontario L2A 5X3. Limit: one entry per envelope. Entries must be sent via 1st-class mail. For eligibility, entries must be received no later than March 31, 1994. No liability is assumed for printing errors, lost, late or misdirected entries.

Sweepstakes is open to persons 18 years of age or older. All applicable laws and regulations apply. Sweepstakes offer void wherever prohibited by law. Prizewinners will be determined no later than May 1994. Chances of winning are determined by the number of entries distributed and received. For a copy of the Official Rules governing this sweepstakes offer, send a self-addressed, stamped envelope (WA residents need not affix return postage) to: Million Dollar Sweepstakes Rules, P.O. Box 4733, Blair, NE 68009.

✂ SD3C

ONE PROOF-OF-PURCHASE
To collect your fabulous FREE GIFT you must include the necessary FREE GIFT proofs-of-purchase with a properly completed offer certificate.

(See inside back cover for offer details)